CITIES
&
WOMEN

CITIES
&
WOMEN

Short Fiction

Hal Howland

**The New
Atlantian Library**

The New Atlantian Library
is an imprint of
ABSOLUTELY AMAZING eBOOKS

Published by Whiz Bang LLC, 926 Truman Avenue, Key West, Florida 33040, USA.

Cities & Women copyright © 2014 by Hal Howland. Electronic compilation/ print editions copyright © 2014 by Whiz Bang LLC. Cover design by Onur Giray. Author photograph by Giovanni Laudicina. This project was made possible in part by a grant from the Anne McKee Artists Fund of the Florida Keys, Inc.

This is a work of fiction. Names, characters, places, and incidents either are the product of the author's imagination or are used fictitiously, and any resemblance to actual persons, living or dead, businesses, companies, events, or locales is entirely coincidental. While the author has made every effort to provide accurate information at the time of publication, neither the publisher nor the author assumes any responsibility for errors, or for changes that occur after publication. Further, the publisher does not have any control over and does not assume any responsibility for author or third-party websites or their contents.

For information contact:
Publisher@AbsolutelyAmazingEbooks.com

ISBN-13: 978-0692202081
ISBN-10: 0692202080

For Jan

ALSO BY HAL HOWLAND

Fiction

After Jerusalem: A Story and Two Novellas (out of print)
The Jazz Buyer: Short Fiction
Landini Cadence and Other Stories: A Rich Castillo Threesome
Murder in Key West (anthology)

Nonfiction

The Human Drummer: Thoughts on the Life Percussive

Jazz Recordings

The Howland Ensemble
Reiko
10 Years in 5 Days

CITIES
&
WOMEN

CONTENTS

Stories

CITIES

From a diary found at Smathers Beach, Key West

Washington, D.C., 1951-59

Smell of acorns, fallen maple leaves in autumn; boxwood, cut grass, red roses in summer. Vague memory of standing with Dad in the George Washington University Hospital parking lot looking up at the window where Mom was holding my newborn brother; I was only three, how could I remember that, but the picture is there. It was also the year that Dad accidentally slammed the car door on my hand at Yellowstone; I don't recall that event or even which hand, but I heard about it for years. First bee sting, right thigh while talking to that girl across the fence who liked to play doctor. School-bus diesel smell, periodic in the suburbs, ever-present in town. Trolleys, Christmas shopping, suspect Santas; lunch with Mom at the S&W Cafeteria. Years later teenage virgins called it the *S&M Cafeteria,* inviting silly images of a cheerful young cashier bent over her supervisor's knee, having intentionally shortchanged a customer for the spanking of her dreams. Hot, humid summers that everyone else hated and I loved; the sad crispness of fall; the bleak suffering of winter, death and stillness on the trees, immobilizing snow pooled as gray slush at your numbed feet, mitigated by Alpine forts and the rosy-cheeked laughter of girls; the gossamer colors of spring, teasing of the sensual heat to come.

Classical LPs and dressed-up concerts and my sister's nascent rock and roll.

"Smoke Gets in Your Eyes"

Miami, 1958

Perpetual summer! *I could live here, oh, yeah.* Smell of coconut oil and every kind of blossom. Our only Christmas in a motel room. Pathetic little fake tree on a coffee table; for years thereafter we kept the tree with the other ornaments in that blue Pullman that smelled of a grandmother's closet. Dinner alfresco at Luigi's, Mom and Dad's favorite. My first case of indigestion, careful with red sauce ever since, despite a generally fearless approach to world cuisine. Spanish red-roofed houses and Spanish street names in Merrick's beloved Coral Gables, the Venetian Pool, unembarrassed tropical profusion, perpetual summer. *Oh, yeah.*

Nutcracker Suite

Tel Aviv, Beirut, 1959-61

Louvered moonlight, sea breeze, distant government gunfire, jackals crying at night. Breakfast of fish, tomatoes, melons, rolls, and orange juice at a beachfront café. Amazing house on a hill, the front at ground level, the back dropping away to a voluptuously fragrant orange grove and a vacant field where snakes and scorpions awaited the distracted walker. Waist-high sprinklers dancing in the arid lawn shaded by pines and eucalyptus. My pal J. and his passion for climbing every tree in our respective yards; his mom calling us down to lemonade and cookies, after we scrubbed fruitlessly at the sap on our hands. The piano, and piano lessons; I preferred the former. Opera, symphonies at Mann Auditorium. Famous visitors in our home, Dad's guests, there to spread the gospel of freedom in a new and not entirely welcome theocracy. A camplike school, detached wood cabins in a dusty, shadowed enclave, not the big brick edifice back home made to look exactly like every other grade school in America. Caesarea, a beach where you could swim and run endlessly without seeing another family, where each of you would claim a small section of silent dunes and search for old Roman coins. I was the first to find one, though all of us did. Dad soaked them in penetrating oil to remove the verdigris. I think my brother has them now. The varied landscapes of Israel, now an oasis of rolling green hills, now a vast Martian valley of death. The long, vertiginous drive to my sister's boarding school in Beirut: narrow cliff-hanging roads, floating seaside cafés, pungent olives, old men gathered in silence around their hookahs, otherworldly wailing music on the radio. That tween girl on the street followed by her *derabucca*-drumming suitor. Hushed visits to Jerusalem, the vibration of massed faith, however misremembered and misused. The souk: falafel in warm pita with tomatoes, onions, and cucumber yogurt, stacked rolls of timeless ornate cloth, primitive brass and copper cookware meant to hang on walls. Smell of spices, roast lamb, overheated people, donkeys, herded sheep, pinecones. Tiberias, Nazareth, Bethlehem, Haifa, Beersheba, seductive Eilat on the Red Sea, biblical ruin upon ruin, epic history nudged forward in a puny wasteland, the site of one arrogant occupation after another. Tel Aviv itself looks like Miami. I could live there too, but Israelis are very picky about their neighbors.

Madama Butterfly

Cairo, Athens, Rome, Paris, 1961
Gorgeous art-lavished tombs, gold masks with made-up eyes that looked right through you, the unfathomable labor of pyramids intercut like gargantuan ant farms, the crumbling Sphinx, the lazy rhythm of a camel ride (our Coptic guide called his beast Canada Dry), astounding museums, a rich and richly superstitious civilization developing math, science, and literature three thousand years before Jesus and his dozen door-to-door salesmen. Custard swimming in burnt caramel syrup in an Agatha Christie dining room. Blue, blue Grecian sea, bluer than anywhere else. The Acropolis, putting the West on notice. Michelangelo's breathtaking Vatican paintings and sculptures. Compared to such sights, the Eiffel Tower resembled an Erector set—but the view from its pinnacle! Echoing Egyptian obelisks in wide-open city parks. The sacred Louvre. Small, graceful hotel rooms with strange bathroom fixtures and stubborn old windows overlooking the city of cities. Smell of fresh-baked bread and more automotive pollution. Washington's uncluttered Parisian skyline trumps its backroom travesties; try telling that to the redneck on the next barstool.

"The Lion Sleeps Tonight"

Washington, D.C., 1961-67
Smell of black walnuts, their chewable stems, and dewy female skin. Music marching forward in my consciousness: vocation, hobby, fun, it drew me in, all

kinds of music. It did battle with swimming and the track-and-field sports I had learned in Israel. Queasy first moments with budding girls, devastating first loves. Impressionable male friends who indulged ridiculous affectations governing how we dressed and behaved, whom we shunned, how we fantasized about girls beyond our reach. J., the would-be Californian who bathed us in the Beach Boys and who lost a radio contest to win a surfboard, which he boasted he would have carried daily through the suburban streets, three thousand miles from the waves to which his spirit called. M., the well-endowed neighbor who was not content merely to describe his newest pastime, masturbation. B., the artist whose dad worked for the CIA and owned a Morris Minor convertible, the same B. who made us hot pastrami sandwiches when we camped in his backyard and with whom on more than one occasion we raced all the way up and down the stairs inside the Washington Monument. R., who called skinny girls *pelicans* (which are anything but skinny) and who wrapped his baby-blue Corvair around a telephone pole and walked away unharmed except by his dad. All those bandmates, at school and in the neighborhood, lavishing equal attention on Sousa, Copland, Count Basie, and the Beatles. All those beautiful musical instruments in catalogs and store windows, some of which I would adopt, several of which I still own. The social earthquakes of JFK, civil rights, women's rights, ecology, Vietnam, a generation gap that itself felt like war. Washington would burn in my next absence, and I wouldn't miss the place.

"Light My Fire"

Paris, 1967

Dad posing for a photograph in the Tuileries, grinning with his hand on a shapely statue's ass, the only lewd act I ever saw him commit, as he tried to cheer up his exiled teenage son. Women on bicycles with phallic baguettes too big for straw baskets.

Sgt. Pepper

Amsterdam, 1967-69 (revisited 1970-71)

My first urban home, though we lived many blocks from downtown. Smell of buttery sugar cookies, *saté* (grilled chicken or pork in Indonesian peanut sauce, spelled *satay* elsewhere), French fries doused in a tart yellow mayonnaise (tastier than *Pulp Fiction* would make it sound), yet more gasoline fumes despite a national passion for the bicycle. The queerest, most charming architecture, a whole country of toy cities that looked like overgrown electric-train layouts. (There is an actual miniature city in The Hague called Madurodam.) Ingenious infrastructure stolen from the sea and, like Venice, slowly sinking back into it. Concentric canals, trams and trains that ran on time, cosmopolitan citizens who spoke better English than most Americans. Season tickets to the glorious Royal Concertgebouw Orchestra, resident about a mile from my house in an iconic hall wherein finally I knew the transcendental nature of music. Vondelpark, the haunt of dads, dogs, moms, babies, students, and lovers. The office-supply store on Beethovenstraat, smelling of glue and ink, where they carefully wrapped your purchase in striped kraft. The only American product available in that shop: the trendy, leaky new Bic pen. Indigenous notebook paper in odd sizes with line spacing that didn't insult your intelligence. We carried our school gear in canvas Dutch army-surplus rucksacks. Everyone I knew lived in a typical row house; ours, given my dad's prestigious position, was a castle. Unforgettable beauty, splendor, luxury. My large room on the third floor, site of numerous teenage rites. Walked and bicycled every inch of that amazing port city, at all hours, never feeling less than perfectly safe. The famous red-light district, superficially more smiling tourist trap than den of iniquity. The whole city dotted with fine restaurants and hip nightclubs. Real jazz, not cocktail music, and the peak of Memphis soul. Enlightened psychedelia long before most Yanks had heard of Haight-Ashbury. Today's "coffee shops" had yet to arrive, but on the street you could buy a block of hashish the size of a Hershey bar for the equivalent of twenty-six dollars. I was less familiar with The Hague, where I attended school, though I walked its own streets many a night after missing the last bus home. The neighboring beach resort, Scheveningen, the grand old convention hall on its boardwalk, a carnival pier, built-in ground-level trampolines on the sand, L. in her green bikini on that rare day warm enough to wear it, and a vast, surreal series of fenced dunes, a former military outpost, where we ignored signs to keep out and roamed and kissed and touched. I met the love of my life in Holland; she, other peers I met there, and I are friends to this day.

"Straight, No Chaser"

Antwerp, Brussels, Le Havre, London, Hamilton (Bermuda), Nassau, Miami, 1968

Brief encounters during a sea adventure described in another diary. Saw the worst parts of important cities I should revisit. No distinctive smells, except in the London public restrooms that were segregated between *European* and *Asiatic*. The latter was a large, undivided empty space with holes in the dirt floor.

"Sunshine of Your Love"

Paris, Brussels, 1969

School theatrical tour. Lunch with J. at a sidewalk café, olive oil glossing her luscious lips. Smell of young red wine, artichokes, and J.'s long brown hair shining in the sun. My buddy M. found a pink bra on the Boulevard Saint-Michel and carried it around all day, much to the shopkeepers' amusement. Belgian farmhouses with thatched roofs. Stopped for a country lunch: warm, simple bread, peasant cheese, and orange soda served at room temperature.

Abbey Road

Harrisonburg, Virginia, 1969-73

Not a city at all, but a small college town in the beautiful Shenandoah Valley. The students felt superior to the "townies." Madison College, now James Madison University, had just gone coed; females outnumbered males seven to one. Four years of music, literature, sex, and illusory love.

Arriaga, *Symphony in D*

Washington, D.C., 1974-2000

More music, literature, sex, illusory love. The dark

period. Many respectable accomplishments, none of which has earned me a dime. Had I not been seduced by jazz, classical music, and novels, I would have moved to Los Angeles, where I would have become rich playing unworthy music I still had the capacity to enjoy. A rich man can indulge all sorts of fantasies involving jazz, classical music, and novels. Still the smell of exhaust, rubber, and asphalt. Millions more people than in my childhood. Intolerable winters, perpetual gridlock. A bloody commercial for reincarnation, the one religious notion I'd like to pretend isn't complete bullshit.

Bernstein, *Serenade*

Montego Bay, Jamaica, 1985

Enough of a city to display the worst poverty I'd seen this side of the Middle East. Governor's Coach into the mountains with D., past Bob Marley's house, dirty children trying to sell you crude wooden figurines of the reggae hero, seawater the color of cut glass, intercourse with D. on the floor near the window fan. The sort of airline whose passengers applaud every landing.

Synchronicity

Miami, 2000-present (occasional visits)

Smell of coconut oil, blossoms, a girlfriend's perfume. South Beach, art deco, fantastic restaurants, gorgeous people, polyglot culture, insane drivers. Carl Hiaasen and his pal Dave Barry, whose column I'd never missed in the *Washington Post*. The best feature of this town for someone who once took for granted his season tickets to the Concertgebouw: the Cleveland Orchestra's annual winter residency. *That's* a band that knows where to have a good time.

Firebird Suite

Key West, 2000-present

I moved here because (1) it was as far into the tropics as I could go and still live in what despite many flaws remains the greatest country in the world, and (2) it was too late in my poor-man's career to go anywhere else. Of course, like Harrisonburg, Key West isn't a city; it's a limestone speck in the middle of the ocean overseen by a dozen wealthy Republicans in the tourism trade who don't give a damn what they do to the environment because one of these days the Keys and much of South Florida (like Venice and Amsterdam) will be underwater. For now *Cayo Hueso* is a pretty little island on which to write books and play a bit of music. Considering the jasmine, the corn silk, the stephanotis, the coconut oil, the rum, the occasional woman's perfume, and the jade sea, the place smells great.

Allegri, *Miserere*

EVIDENCE

At least two women own provocative photographs of me naked. That is, I assume they still own them: the first woman in the vain hope of using her evidence against me, the second in memory of our love. Today the three of us live thousands of miles from one another and from the place where we spent our youth.

The first photo resulted from erotic impulse. The woman's older sister, to whom she confessed everything and who was openly curious about our sex life—though she never flirted with me, out of loyalty to her sibling and to her small-town Catholic standards—had bought us a Polaroid camera to play with during an upcoming weekend at the beach. This was long before automated film developing, cell phones, sexting, the popular acceptance of pornography, and the general breakdown of modesty that parades on every urban street. We giggled at the gift and promised to share only those of the resulting images that her sister's community would deem appropriate.

What for my girlfriend was a weekend getaway was for me the middle of a month-long theatrical engagement at a Delaware seaside resort, performing repertory for sunburned secretaries, working-class Baltimore families, and political figures from Washington. I had driven all the way back home to Philadelphia to pick her up and was rewarded on the return drive by the frequent presence of her hand in my pants and of mine in hers.

At the beach we shared a two-bedroom condominium with two other couples: the preoccupied director and his wife and the womanizing lead actor and the wife who by mutual agreement visited only with advance notice. I slept on a daybed in the living room and, having learned to anticipate being invaded, kept my boxers on. At noon on Saturday the other four made a show of leaving for a day on the sand and the boardwalk, to give us some privacy. Apparently we had done little to conceal our mutual hunger. As they were leaving, the star turned to me and said we were welcome to use their room, in case the group returned earlier than expected. I had seen him leering at my girlfriend and suspected that he was interested less in the possibility of catching us making love in the living room than in knowing that she would have done so in his bed.

After brunch she and I showered and joined each other in the actor's room. She was wearing only a tiny pair of sheer black lace panties. We embraced warmly, luxuriating in our clean scents and our tight young bodies. Feeling my rising erection, she brushed my chest with her firm nipples. Instead of our usual immediate tumble into bed, we separated and looked each other up and down. She smiled and whispered, "Get the camera."

Faced suddenly with the prospect of preserving our nakedness for all time, we laughed nervously and wondered aloud how candidly or professionally we wished to present ourselves. I suppose the omnipresence of female nudity in art through the centuries, the fact that she had voiced the suggestion, and the understanding that she was the only person in the world who admired her figure more than I did led us to assume that she would pose first.

I took several shots of her on and around the bed, the best of which showed her reclining Roman-style on her right elbow, her right leg extended toward me and her left raised and bent so that she was boldly exposed. She thoughtfully had shaved for the occasion. Like most of my girlfriends, she had small breasts that looked good in any position (and that would age much more gracefully than the pendulous hooters most men seem to crave, a trait I have always found comically Oedipal). Her left hand rested at her side. Dangling from her right hand, draped like a creamy blossom across her pillow, were the panties she had thrown there. Her long, straight brown hair cascaded invisibly behind her to afford a complete frontal view. She directed her placid gaze away from the lens, both to give the scene a look of intriguing disinterest and to prevent the red-eye effect we knew we could expect from our cheap camera. She was gorgeous, and I would treasure that photograph for years.

When it was my turn to pose, she ordered me to stand backed against the wall so I could be seen both straight on and reflected in the full-length mirror angled to my left. She told me to touch myself lightly with my fingertips, and she watched long enough to require further instruction guaranteeing the suggestion of masturbation without my actually hiding anything. She photographed me while kneeling on the carpet, presumably to make me look bigger (she had missed no opportunity to point out that she had experienced larger penises than mine). By now I was visibly wet, and she complained of being unable to capture that shiny harbinger while fitting my whole body in the frame. She told me to look to the side, producing a twin profile. She snapped three shots and cranked them out without inspection. Finally she chose her favorite and studied it for several seconds. "Mmmm," she smiled.

We wrapped the rejected prints in the morning newspaper and stashed the bundle at the bottom of the kitchen trash container.

We spent the rest of the weekend making love, arguing, realizing we were platonically incompatible, and regretting our acquaintance. The drive back to Philly was long and tense, and when we parted we assumed it was forever. We were so disenchanted by the time I placed her suitcase on her porch that we did not even think to ask each other to return those photographs. We had left the camera in the beachside condo to which I would return the next day.

We reunited several times over the years, having acknowledged that sex was the only language we could speak together.

During one of her visits, she was sitting at my tidy desk, moving things about trying to get a rise out of me while I sat on the floor at her feet (a physical arrangement she would have regarded as natural and fitting). She twirled around in the chair a few times and suddenly fixed me with her inescapable sky-blue eyes. "Whatever did you do with that nude photo you took of me in Rehoboth?" she asked with mock innocence.

"I still have it, of course," I admitted foolishly. "It's right there in that drawer."

She pulled out the writing-table section of my mission-oak antique and lifted the lid. That her lovely photograph was the only object in the drawer undoubtedly thrilled her. She picked it up and stared at it for a minute or so under the warm lamplight. Then she carefully tore it apart, preserving just the depiction of her face. She ripped the rest of the print into small pieces and dumped them in her purse. "There," she smiled. "You get to keep the best part."

At the time, the image of her fantastic body was burned into my consciousness with such clarity that I did not rush to stop her from destroying what I considered a beautiful work of art (her pose, not the lame snapshot itself). When I protested and assured her that I would never have shared the photo with anyone, she replied that life was too uncertain to let such damning evidence exist where it would be discovered should I get hit by a bus. She claimed that she had long before discarded her nude photo of me, ostensibly for the same reason. (I doubt she would have thought to spare the feelings of an inquisitive boyfriend.)

I still have the vandalized corner of my photo of her; I keep it to remind me of our brief happiness. I remember the rest all too well.

The other woman who presumably still owns naked pictures of me is as dear to my heart as on the day we were introduced. We had a sweet courtship and a joyous, imaginative sex life, based on a deep abiding friendship. Moving in together when I was still too young and insatiable to refuse brief encounters with other girls proved to be a mistake, however, and gradually I grew immune to her.

We too reconciled years later. Unlike her predecessor, though, she realized that sex would never be enough to sustain us. We remained friends and, via e-mail, have walked each other through numerous other relationships and personal crises. Her naughty photographs of me were products of our earliest days.

About a month into our intimacy I was booked on the road with another troupe for several weeks, and she and I poured out our libidinous yearning in lengthy letters. Shyness and the poverty of our youth precluded our indulging in long-distance phone sex. But in one of her bodice rippers she asked me to take some nude photographs of myself strictly for her personal pleasure, using the old-fashioned Polaroid camera she had seen in my apartment. I happened to have the cumbersome device with me on the road, since the company was performing in a picturesque region and at the time I did not own a smaller and better camera.

I gladly satisfied the request. I took two shots of myself naked and hard in the bathroom mirror of my hotel room, one straight on and one in profile (she had remarked on how pretty my erection was from a certain angle). The flash and the bulk of the camera itself concealed my face. I had no reason to suspect that these photos would ever fall into the wrong hands and, their anonymity notwithstanding, would never have begrudged my friend's enjoying them however she wished.

I visited a local office-supply store, bought a photo mailer, and sent the prints to my girl. She wrote back that they were delicious and described various things she had done with herself while viewing them.

When I returned from the tour and visited her apartment I found the photos mounted in full view in the frame of her vanity mirror. She sat there cooing at them and reapplying red lipstick while I stood behind her with my vertical cock entwined in her soft blonde hair.

I am not at all convinced that the first woman ever actually destroyed her smoking gun; selfishness and duplicity were her most reliable characteristics. But I will not flatter either of us with the notion that she could have any reason to exploit it, since (1) a bit of research on her part would confirm that I have nothing, financial or otherwise, that she could want; (2) we have not exchanged a word in many years; and (3) she recently celebrated a very public wedding to a fat Episcopal priest young enough to be her daughter.

As for her opposite, I hope she has kept her photos in a cool, dry place. I hope she takes them out occasionally and thinks of us. I must remember to ask, before it is too late.

THE GRAND TOUR

In memory of Colette (1873-1954)

In the fall of 1976, Washington, D.C., drummer Adrian Edwards found himself between gigs and treading water as a clerk at a chain music store in a shopping mall in suburban Vienna, Virginia. This was one of those generic dealerships that catered to piano teachers, school-band directors, and families buying their first piano or organ. Asian manufacturers of musical instruments and electronics were now beating the pants off the American firms, whose quality control had hit rock bottom. (Nostalgic musicians who seek out "vintage" American gear from the seventies are for the most part fooling themselves.) The few guitars, drums, and other "hip" instruments on the premises were aimed squarely at students, and no professional musician liked being seen in the place. The polyester-clad keyboard salespeople spent most of their time standing around waiting to ambush Mom and Dad as they dragged in little Ricky to smudge the shiny second-rate pianos. What kept the business running was the sale of instructional books and sheet music, and that was Adrian Edwards's department.

The job was easy, orderly, educational, and temporary. Adrian of course had not told his employer that he had no desire make a career out of selling method books, or that he already had accepted a gig with a show band whose national tour was to begin the following spring. Adrian's supervisor, Tom Cavendish, was a graduate art student, a few years younger than Adrian, who entertained two disparate vocations: avant-garde painting and country blues. The guy could grab a crummy guitar off the wall and make it sound exactly like the crummy guitar Robert Johnson had schlepped out to the crossroads. The job's only felicity for Adrian was a brief dalliance with fellow clerk Tania Estienne, who had attended art school with Tom. The affair began fittingly on the day the three took in a witty Robert Rauschenberg exhibit in the afternoon and a jarring evening performance by the Twentieth-Century Consort. The affair and the job ended when Adrian split to go on the road.

The show band was one of the first groups Adrian would join whose members were completely new to him; they hailed from all around the Beltway. The music director, Al Beale, who had gotten Adrian's number from another bandleader, was also the group's bassist and onstage sound engineer: a bad combination, since that meant the bottom would drop out of the music every time the guy turned around to adjust the mixing board.

Adrian's audition had been an after-hours cattle call at a Crystal City restaurant, where all the candidates played on the house equipment. Adrian had awaited his turn in the lobby with a semifamous local guitarist who admitted he had no intention of joining the band but had shown up simply for a laugh; he spent the entire session playing fancy licks that would never have been tolerated in a floor show. Adrian's more sincere musicianship won him the drum chair—somewhat to his surprise, since the uncomfortable drum set consisted of four deadened tubs and a dozen beat-up cymbals, the only musical one of which was just out of reach. It was at this audition that Adrian met the star of the show, a mediocre Vegas-type crooner named Gus Tormé. Adrian did not bother to ask how often Gus was assumed to be related to Mel Tormé, which unfortunately he was not.

The first rehearsal took place on a freezing winter night in Gus's ranch house just off Georgia Avenue in Silver Spring, Maryland. The thin, bespectacled young man who answered Adrian's knock at the door with, "So, who the hell are you?" turned out to be the newly hired guitarist, Kevin Gainsborough. Apparently no one had told Kevin that the previous drummer had been on indefinite probation. Kevin and Adrian nonetheless would become lifelong friends and in later years would perform together in other groups.

The rest of the band consisted of a brilliant nineteen-year-old keyboardist aptly named Bob Beckstein, who had cut his teeth illegally in Baltimore strip clubs, and two attractive young female backup singers, brunette Linda Sun and blonde Jane Corning. The women, Kevin, and Adrian were in their middle to late twenties; Gus and Al were just past thirty. All the accompanists were hoping to break out of the unimaginative D.C. commercial scene, and all recognized that touring with an extremely commercial show band was unlikely to provide the escape they sought. The seven musicians found themselves in the same room only because they had been promised the biggest weekly paycheck any of them had ever earned. Each of the guys already owned a black tuxedo for weeknights and did not complain when Al escorted them to a nearby mall to be fitted for a white tux to wear on Friday and Saturday nights.

The show opened with a two-week engagement at a Holiday Inn in Fredericksburg, Virginia, a mere hour southwest of D.C. Gus had chosen the nearby debut just in case someone in the band turned out to be a maniac and had to be replaced before the show continued on to the next stop, Philadelphia.

The group traveled in three vehicles: Gus's unassuming white Toyota sedan in the lead, followed by Al's old blue Chevy van, with Adrian's newer red Ford van bringing up the rear. In the wake of Vietnam and Watergate, no one had commented on the accidentally patriotic color scheme. Kevin and Bob would take turns riding with Gus or Al. The latter carried all the band gear except Adrian's drum set, which rode in his own van along with the backup singers' considerable wardrobes. The women were the least experienced band members and therefore the least road-savvy; after a few weeks of travel Adrian relied entirely on his exterior mirrors to see around two mountains of dresses that had outgrown their containers. Gus had driven to Fredericksburg in the company of his girlfriend, a pretty brunette named Amy Villard who had hoped to join the entourage as Gus's road manager. The couple was prone to loud and occasionally violent arguments, however, and no one was surprised when the group departed Fredericksburg without Amy. The others assumed the two had broken up or had taken a breather, but few had expected to see singer Linda Sun slide onto Gus's passenger seat as the convoy prepared to hit the highway. Jane later admitted to Adrian that toward the end of the Fredericksburg gig Linda had relocated from their shared hotel room to Gus's.

During rehearsals, Adrian had taken a protective liking to Jane, a married high-school English teacher whose older husband, David, had encouraged Jane to seize this opportunity to realize her musical dreams. Adrian, a former English major, invited Jane to ride with him on the first leg of the tour, specifically in hopes of talking her out of this unpromising fantasy. He figured he could relate enough professional horror stories in the first two hours to convince Jane that she had made a mistake and should call David to rescue her before the group got too far from home. Adrian would fail in this brotherly mission and later would be glad of it.

What Gus's New York agent, Herb Singer, had meant by Philadelphia was actually suburban Cherry Hill, New Jersey. Years later Adrian would remember his fortnight at the Polynesian Palace as a deleted nightmare sequence from *GoodFellas*. The Gus Tormé Show performed nightly in the main room and, during happy hour, endured a reduced setup in a smaller lounge on the other side of the building. The whole staff was right out of central casting. Adrian and Jane were understandably conflicted over the fact that by the end of the Cherry Hill gig their friendship had turned secretly sexual.

One of the curiosities of nineteen seventies male fashion was the wearing of skintight trousers that left little to the imagination, thus teaching novice female observers that most men have much less to show than popular culture would suggest. One day Gus, Al, and Adrian were walking back from lunch when they encountered a tall, handsome man coming their way with what looked like a juvenile elephant's trunk in his pants. The three musicians pretended not to notice. But as soon as the guy passed them, Gus launched into a speech on the fallacies of penile functionality—after which Al and Adrian never looked at their front man in quite the same way.

Herb Singer was a likable middle-aged fellow who actually appreciated good music but otherwise was a typical agent. He managed a stable of show bands all over the country and sent them wherever it was most convenient for him. He would turn up on the last night of Gus's engagements and tell the band that their previously scheduled next gig had evaporated and that now they were going somewhere else, usually hundreds of miles farther on. From Cherry Hill they were to drive not to Hartford, Connecticut, but rather to Hyannis, Massachusetts—and they had just enough time to get there, check in, set up, miss dinner, maybe take a shower, and play the first of thirteen consecutive nightly shows.

One of Adrian's private amusements was making up silly lyrics to popular songs. "What I Did for Love," from the musical *A Chorus Line,* was a nightly feature of Gus's act. After a few months on the road, Adrian shared with the others his version:

What I Did for Herb

Kiss my ass goodbye
And point me toward Toledo
Wish me luck, and save my mail
No, I can't forget

What I did for Herb
What I did for Herb

Look, my eyes are red
And now we're out of NoDoz
If we rush we won't get docked
Man, is this a crock
Why do I deserve
What I did for Herb

Gone, my check is always gone
And as we travel on
It's Herb that we'll remember

Kiss my ass goodbye
The sleazy, smelly truck stops
You would think I'd know by now
He said, Sign here
And now I fear
I sold my rear
For Herb
What I did for Herb
What I did for Herb

The happy moments in Hyannis occurred during the daytime, when band members would break off in twos or threes, check out the beaches—though the spring weather was far too cold for swimming—enjoy fresh seafood, and try to catch glimpses of the Kennedy compound.

For the first few stops, Adrian found himself rooming with young Bob Beckstein, whose mechanical knowledge of the Hammond B-3 organ rose to the level of poetry. In conversation Bob could make the electrical journey from the keyboard out to the Leslie rotating-speaker cabinet sound like the *Odyssey* itself. Bob's passion for Afro-Cuban music was a mixed blessing, however, since the versatile young player missed no opportunity to practice on his deafening Gretsch timbales. Everyone's ears rejoiced when Bob's parents called one day to report that their son had been chosen to play piano in a Tommy Dorsey tribute band. Weeks later Bob would be replaced by another young D.C. keyboardist who had auditioned for Gus the same night as Bob—but not before Bob relayed to his roommate on the last night of the Hyannis gig that the Gus Tormé Show was traveling from there not to Boston but rather to Detroit. This time the band did not make the ridiculous drive in time and had to forfeit their first night's pay.

The Detroit gig was distinguished by two opposites: (1) the nicest hotel on the tour, complete with indoor pools, hot tubs, saunas, and luxurious bedrooms; and (2) the dinner at which Adrian foolishly ordered lobster, many leagues from the sea, and contracted food poisoning. The band took their violently ill drummer to the hospital emergency room for a shot, and he spent most of two days in bed. Fortunately Bob's start date with "Tommy Dorsey" had been postponed, and he was able to fill in on the drums during Adrian's worst night of explosive dehydration.

Adrian's friendship with guitarist Kevin Gainsborough deepened when the drummer began rooming with him. Kevin was easygoing and quick to laugh, with no annoying habits and more musicianship than he could ever use with Gus's outfit. Kevin, like nearly every other American, had become a fan of comedian Steve Martin, whose appearances on *The Tonight Show* and *Saturday Night Live* had turned the goofy banjo-wielding former magician into an international sensation. Whenever Kevin felt like sharing a joint with Adrian, he would quote Martin: *"Hey, man, let's get small!"* The two musicians shared hilarious conversations about their lounge-lizard employer; one night Gus overheard one of these and for the rest of the tour kept his guitarist and drummer at a polite distance.

After a few months on the road, Gus's volatile personality had put a strain on his fling with Linda Sun. Almost immediately thereafter, Gus's girlfriend Amy Villard rejoined the tour. The others tolerated the couple's frequent fights, one of which occurred during a sound check and saw the star impotently punching the curtain and throwing his expensive white microphone to the stage floor. Ever the faithful sidekick, Al Beale quickly reached into a flight case and produced a shiny new replacement.

Linda went back to sleeping in Jane's hotel room and confessed that she expected both of them to be fired: Herb or someone else had convinced Gus that the guys in the band could sing the girls' parts as well as anyone and that what the act really needed was not backup singers but rather backup dancers. During the weeks when this rumor circulated, Adrian and Jane's affair had become common knowledge. Adrian often would sleep with Jane while Linda kept her back turned on the opposite side of the room. The others began assuming that Adrian, Linda, and Jane were carrying on a ménage à trois. This was not true, but the three did not go out of their way to spoil the illusion.

Linda Sun had been a rock singer and was a bit earthier than her bookish onstage partner. Linda had taken to riding with Adrian and Jane and often indulged a surprising fetish: mooning people. Construction workers, men and women driving beside the caravan, and of course Adrian and Jane themselves became intimately familiar with Linda's athletic lower half. The two wordsmiths would joke about *Sun* and her *Moon*. This playful nonsense was innocuous until the night when Adrian, Jane, Linda, and an old boyfriend of Linda's found themselves stoned, making love in their separate hotel beds a few feet apart, and occasionally calling out the wrong name. Fortunately, the two couples, unlike Gus, were apt to forgive the hallucinogenic effects of good marijuana.

As Linda had feared, the two backup singers were replaced by nearly identical backup dancers, the brunette conveniently turning out to be Gus's girlfriend, Amy. Linda, from whom everyone had learned to expect the unexpected, returned to her childhood home in Shepherdstown, West Virginia, and rejoined her old rock band. Jane returned to D.C., resumed teaching, and prepared to divorce her well-meaning avuncular husband; she and Adrian corresponded by lusty letters.

The tour eventually took the weary survivors to Providence; an amusement park in Agawam, Massachusetts, evoked to perfection years later in *This Is Spinal Tap;* the actual Philadelphia; a honeymoon resort in the Poconos, where Adrian observed presidential brother Billy Carter in the company of a gorgeous young woman who appeared to be a rental; back to D.C.; down to Tampa; and on to parts unknown. During the brief visit home, Kevin Gainsborough had learned that a revered local folk-rocker with major-label interest was seeking a new guitarist and a new drummer. Kevin and Adrian spent their two weeks in Tampa anticipating their freedom from the Gus Tormé Show.

On stage one night in Tampa, Adrian heard himself play an astounding polyrhythmic drum fill that he had never heard anyone play and that would have done credit to Tony Williams himself. Such a rare and miraculous moment would in the years ahead remain Adrian's primary reason for struggling on as a musician.

Having received his two tarnished sidemen's notice, Gus brought down a semiprofessional drummer friend to rehearse with the band during the daytime so he could make a more or less smooth transition when Adrian left. Gus had resolved to do without a guitarist for the time being, thus putting a heavier weight on the already overburdened young keyboardist who had replaced Bob. Eventually Gus prevailed on Adrian to let the new drummer play with the band during one of the shows and asked Adrian to sit in the audience and take notes. Adrian found a seat at a front-row table in the sparsely populated room and dutifully jotted down anything that might boost the clumsy percussionist's confidence. At one point between verses plucked from the Great American Songbook, Gus walked over to Adrian's table, grabbed his pen and notebook, and laughingly wrote *FUCK YOU!* The new drummer obviously was not going to last long; when

Adrian departed the band near Washington, Gus was quick to admit that he would miss him.

Adrian Edwards's affair with Jane Corning resumed with abandon on Adrian's return home. The musical veteran who had tried to dissuade Jane from deserting her English students was no less surprised by her divorce, or by his deepening love for her. The two eventually lived together for several years, until Adrian's favorite high-school sweetheart reappeared out of the blue and caused yet another upheaval for the trusting former backup singer. Jane and Adrian managed to reclaim their friendship years later. Jane's biggest and happiest surprise for Adrian came when she suddenly moved to Nashville, where she blossomed into a widely respected blues artist.

Kevin Gainsborough's own good intentions came to nothing when it turned out that the promising songwriter he and Adrian were planning to join together had already chosen another guitarist. Adrian spent three glorious years with the lovable hippies who made up the eclectic Robert Sellers Band, which eventually collapsed under the weight of a clueless record industry that valued sex appeal above art. Today Kevin Gainsborough remains one of the top two or three guitarists in the nation's capital, for what that is worth.

Gus Tormé made a feeble attempt to continue touring with the remnants of his band but eventually gave up and returned to Silver Spring. He was never heard from again.

GROUNDED ON GARBAGE

Stephan Schemel, an Orlando attorney who was among one hundred twenty-four passengers aboard Superior Airlines Flight 4012 from Atlanta's Hartsfield International Airport to Donald Duck International Airport in Orlando on January 12, 2014, said that as soon as the plane touched down the pilot applied the brake very forcibly. Schemel was wearing a seatbelt but lurched forward because of the heavy braking. He reported smelling burnt rubber as the plane was stopping.

Donald Duck International has a runway that is more than seven thousand feet long, a typical size for commercial traffic. The longest runway at nearby Mel Blanc Municipal Airport is only slightly more than three thousand feet because it is designed for small private planes.

After the jet stopped, a flight attendant welcomed passengers to Orlando, Schemel said. Then, after a few moments, the pilot came on and admitted that he had landed at the wrong airport.

Superior spokeswoman Brie Klein said grounding the

two pilots involved was common while the airline and federal aviation officials investigated the mistake. The captain was in his fifteenth year flying for Superior, Klein said.

At first, Schemel said, he considered the mistake only an inconvenience. But once he got off the plane, someone pointed to the edge of the runway, which he estimated as about a hundred feet away. The lawyer's opinion of the incident as a business opportunity was not known.

Mike Pendleton, manager of the smaller airport, described the distance as closer to three hundred feet. He said the runway was built on a landfill. At the end there is a significant drop-off, with a ravine beneath it, then Florida's Turnpike on the other side. He said a Boeing 737 had never landed at Mel Blanc Municipal, which opened in 1969 and normally handled light jets, turboprops, and small aircraft for the charter, corporate, and tourism markets.

Mel Blanc Municipal was deserted when the Superior flight landed. Airport staffers had gone home about an hour earlier but were called back after the unexpected arrival, Pendleton said.

Boris Hechinger, a spokesman for Houston-based Superior, said everyone aboard the jet was safe. He did not know why the plane went to the wrong airport.

Federal Aviation Administration spokesman Tim Michaels said the agency was investigating, but he declined to elaborate.

James Bickel, executive director of Donald Duck International, said the Superior pilot was in communication with the airport tower, which cleared him to land around six in the evening. The plane touched down a few minutes later at the other field. Skies were clear at the time, with the temperature in the seventies, Bickel said.

Passengers were loaded on buses for the seven-mile trip to Orlando. Superior brought in another, smaller plane for passengers who were flying on to Miami. That flight departed around ten o'clock that night.

Hechinger expected the aircraft involved in the mistaken landing to be able to take off from the smaller runway. The minimum runway length needed to take off varies, depending on a plane's weight, the outside temperature, and other factors. Boeing documents state that a lightly loaded 737 can take off from a runway about the length of that at Mel Blanc Municipal. In case that turned out to be too dangerous to attempt, Superior offered to move their expensive jet out of the way and convert it to a restaurant or an aviation museum, assuming the aircraft had not ended up in pieces on the turnpike.

Instances of commercial jets landing at the wrong airport are unusual but not unheard-of, according to pilots and aviation safety experts. Usually the pilots are flying "visually," that is, without the aid of the automatic pilot, in clear weather. The instances typically involve low-traffic airports situated close together with runways aligned to the same or similar compass points.

This brings to mind the old Bob Newhart bit where the captain of a no-frills flight bound for Honolulu comes back to the cabin to chat with passengers, asks whether any of them has ever been to the big island of Hawaii, and says,

"It's kind of pear-shaped, isn't it?"

It is unlikely that this problem would occur between John F. Kennedy and LaGuardia airports, or Newark and LaGuardia, said former National Transportation Safety Board member Jack Genovese, referring to three New York-area airports. Planes approaching such busy destinations are under total air-traffic control until they come down to about five hundred feet. Wrong-airport landings have happened about twice a year for the past several years, Genovese said. Safety experts believe there are many more instances of planes that *almost* land at the wrong airport when the pilot realizes the mistake and aborts the landing in time.

In the recent Florida case, a key question for investigators was why the second Superior pilot, who was not flying the plane, did not catch the error in time to prevent the mistaken landing. Typically, the copilot is supposed to monitor navigation aids and other aircraft systems. Later it was rumored that at the time of the landing the copilot and one of the flight attendants were having sex in the first-class lavatory.

Popular culture produced another relevant examination of this issue in the 2012 Denzel Washington film *Flight,* in which an alcoholic pilot expertly lands a disabled jetliner in an open field despite being drunk and high on cocaine. The much younger copilot, who had expressed doubts about his partner's fitness to fly, wakes in a hospital bed paralyzed and credits Jesus Christ for his survival.

The January 2014 event was the second time in less than two months that a large jet had landed at the wrong airport. In November 2013, a freight-carrying Boeing 747 that was supposed to deliver parts to McConnell Air Force Base in Wichita, Kansas, landed nine miles north at Colonel James Jabara Airport. The company that operated the flight said later in a training video that the crew was skeptical about the plane's automation after the copilot's flight display had malfunctioned; the pilot chose to fly visually and then spotted the brightly lit runway at Jabara. Earlier that year a cargo plane bound for MacDill Air Force Base in Tampa had landed without incident at the small Peter O. Knight Airport nearby. An investigation blamed confusion identifying airports in the area, and base officials introduced an updated landing procedure.

Perhaps the most infamous Florida aircraft diversion occurred in 1964, when the Beatles were traveling to a concert in Jacksonville and were forced to fly around Hurricane Dora; they landed eventually on the short white-knuckle runway in far distant Key West. Investigators reported later that the band's chartered four-prop Lockheed L-188 Electra had an unenviable safety record. To occupy their time during the unplanned layover, the "boys" were driven to Miami, where they had partied before and after their second set of performances on the *Ed Sullivan Show,* taped at the Deauville Hotel. Today the former Key Wester Resort cottage where the Beatles stayed briefly is an open-air bar called the Abbey Road Snack Shack, on the grounds of the Hyatt Windward Pointe Resort. Patrons can purchase such items as the I Want to Hold Your Ham Sandwich, the Lovely MargaRita, and Aunt Mimi's Saltpeter Biscuits in a handsome collectible tin. Bar employees report that they are completely sold out of the vials of pool water and tiny squares cut from sheets, towels, and other items that the Fab Four may have touched during their visit.

THE HIJACKING
OF THE
DAVE MANDARINE
BAND

Dave Mandarine was among the finest electric guitarists in Baltimore by the time he was twenty years old. He achieved his grittily beautiful tone simply by overdriving a small Fender amplifier with one cable and two expert hands. To get something approaching this sound, most of Dave's peers required a Marshall stack, a maze of pedals, and an excruciating volume level. That Dave could read standard notation and tablature spared him the old jazz musician's joke: *How do you get a guitarist to turn down? Put a piece of music in front of him!* Dave's main ax was a stock Stratocaster of unremarkable lineage, though on occasion he could be seen bearing the considerable weight of an ancient Gibson Les Paul. Dave's unerring sense of melody gave his improvised solos musical substance found lacking in more than a few rock stars' pyrotechnics. Dave's mastery of fingerpicking, flatpicking, and slide (in the absence of which device he was glad to substitute a nightclub patron's handy beer bottle) would have assured him a full-time career in the studios of Los Angeles, had he ever developed a desire to live there. The guitarist's vague resemblance to Eric Clapton earned him a steady stream of envious male comments and libidinous female advances; he modestly deflected the former and eagerly welcomed the latter. By his thirties Dave Mandarine had played every kind of rock and pop gig in town, from tuxedoed agency bands and local heroes' backup groups to a succession of his own crack outfits. Dave doubled as a respected guitar teacher. He had learned to laugh off the local media's tendency to misspell his surname, French for *tangerine,* and did not seem to mind that he had exhausted his hometown's creative possibilities.

Dave Mandarine's father had been a naval officer—the future musician was actually born in Japan and would speak bits of several languages before graduating from high school—and had instilled in his son an itching wanderlust as well as an interest in all things nautical. Less promising was Dave's inherited weakness for alcohol. In 1994 the three traits came together in the form of an impulsive road trip, the only plan for which was to fuck and drink his way from Baltimore to Key West.

Almost immediately on arriving in the Southernmost City, Dave Mandarine landed a house gig leading a rocking trio at Martha Gellhorn's Tavern, a Greene Street bar renamed for the spot where Ernest Hemingway had met his future third wife. The club's motto, *A Clean, Well-Lighted Place*—the cavelike establishment was neither— brought a smile to the rare visitor whose familiarity with Hemingway's iconic output was more than a scholastic memory. Without the two writers' association, the dilapidated old building half a block off the main drag, Duval Street, would have faced the same uncertain future as any of Key Weird's many other watering holes.

For the previous few decades Martha Gellhorn's had thrived under the ownership of a locally famous character named Sal Ricci, whose reputation as a womanizer, gambler, smuggler, gunrunner, angler, and raconteur was nearly as colorful as that of Papa Hemingway himself. A brief, tiring foray into municipal politics and declining health had reduced the club owner to the role of beloved figurehead, greeting patrons from a barstool in the doorway, posing for photographs, and indulging in sexual innuendo that would have earned a younger man a well-deserved slap in the face. In exchange for this pleasant retirement Ricci turned the bar over to a tall, energetic newcomer from Wyoming whose interest in literary history took a backseat to an insatiable hunger for money.

Kenny Schuster stood at six feet, four inches and automatically ducked his head many times a night as he negotiated the various archways and alcoves that remained of the building's previous incarnations. His meticulously greased black hair and high-top sneakers gave Schuster the appearance of a nineteen fifties basketball star, an effect that was spoiled up close by the realization that the club owner wore tattooed eye makeup. Throughout the evening Schuster was everywhere at once, checking the till and ensuring that his bartenders were pouring the stingiest drinks in town.

Schuster displayed a worshipful respect for celebrity that manifested itself primarily in a famous name painted in large yellow letters atop every barstool in the club. Apparently personages from Leonard Bernstein to Robert De Niro had planted their asses on those stools at some point over the years. Schuster could keep a listener occupied for some time with stories of after-hours parties during which he had shared joints and lines of coke with A-list visitors from around the globe. Most of the tales were true; few of them were interesting. Less engaging still was the businessman's tendency to veer without warning into passages of confrontational right-wing punditry.

Kenny Schuster's greed surfaced most offensively in his relations with Dave Mandarine's band. Not only did the proprietor pay the musicians the same lousy money Dave had earned twenty years earlier in Baltimore, Schuster would actually wager against the group's tips. If Dave won the coin toss, Schuster would double the usually negligible amount of money in the onstage tip jar; if Schuster won, the band received no tips at all. Dave had never encountered this unsavory tactic anywhere before, but the need to retain his steady gig and the increasingly obvious effects of his alcoholism kept the guitarist from objecting to Schuster's rude pastime.

Even more obnoxious was Schuster's willingness to advise Dave regarding his choice of sidemen. Not content to leave bandleading to the bandleader, Schuster would judge every bass player and every drummer according to his potential to tickle the cash register. If the player could sing well or motivate the audience, he was welcome to stay; someone who merely played the hell out of his instrument was just taking up space. Dave was loathe to argue with this additional interference because (1) he too realized that musicianship alone was insufficient to populate the dance floor, and (2) he acknowledged that his own static stage presence and undistinguished vocal ability could use all the window dressing they could get. Dave's worldwide reputation rested solely on his phenomenal guitar playing. The result was that Dave's band experienced an unnecessarily high turnover; by the year 2000 every bassist and drummer in town had shared the Gellhorn's stage with Dave for a few nights, months, or, in rare cases, years. Dave's impressive repertoire comprised hundreds of cover songs and a few originals, but no rhythm section had ever played all of them—and usually they underwent simplified arrangements that could be pulled off without rehearsal. The average Key West musician was a lazy dropout who regarded the *R* word with disdain. Dave's winking welcome speech to a new sideman was, "We play everything just like the record, and we never make a mistake."

One of the Baltimore musicians with whom Dave Mandarine had stayed in contact was Isaac "Ike" Ireton, a Peabody Conservatory graduate who played world-class flute, clarinet, and saxophone in numerous mid-Atlantic jazz and classical groups. For fun, Ireton had taught himself to play tasteful, rock-steady drums. He enjoyed a second career as a writer of novels, short stories, and musical nonfiction. Having realized that he too had run out of new things to do in the oppressively congested Baltimore-Washington area, and having long before lost his taste for raking leaves and shoveling snow, Ireton decided in the millennial year to accept Dave's invitation to check out the end of the road. Ireton packed his horns, drums, and downsized household effects and headed south.

Since above-average musicians were precious

commodities in Key West, Ike too was booked solid before he had finished unpacking. He could have contented himself with being practically the only decent reedman in town, but he spent equal time behind his drum kit. Whenever Dave Mandarine's regular drummer was unavailable—the disagreeable, unmusical player maintained a sideline as an incompetent audio engineer— Ike reluctantly agreed to endure a night or two behind the worst sounding drums he had ever heard. Ike's admiration for Dave's playing and the two musicians' hometown backgrounds ameliorated the fact that Ike had outgrown his friend's repertoire and was there just for the joy of playing the drums. Since Ike sang lead and backup as well as anyone in the Keys, bassists, bar staff, and patrons welcomed his occasional presence at Gellhorn's.

Whenever a listener or Ike Ireton himself broached the subject of replacing Dave Mandarine's tiresome drummer, the leader displayed a cautious loyalty that was at once respectable and incomprehensible.

"I just can't justify firing someone without reason," Dave would say.

How about the fact that he can't play or sing, for starters? Ike would wonder.

This curious situation continued for a full ten years, during which Ike became Dave's first-call sub drummer and learned more than his share of the vast Mandarine songlist. Ike's own vocal repertoire contributed sophistication and variety that club owner Kenny Schuster could not ignore.

One of the many bassists who had put in the odd appearance with Dave Mandarine at Martha Gellhorn's was Juan Bautista Sanchez, a fiftyish Miami egomaniac who had burned so many bridges in his city of five and a half million that he gladly traveled to tiny Key West every weekend to find work. He walked the length of Duval Street nearly twenty-four hours a day harassing club owners and musicians and thus had secured a handful of freelance accounts.

To say that Sanchez specialized in nineteen seventies funk would be an understatement. He knew and cared about no other repertoire and seized every opportunity to say so. For years in Miami he had led a cheesy show band called Summer Wind that he brought occasionally to Key West for special events. The local scene was so unpolished that Sanchez could sell Summer Wind as a headlining act, despite the fact that most members of Sanchez's generation had not bothered with seventies funk since dancing to it at their wedding receptions. Sanchez could name the individual members of every one-dimensional band from Cameo to Kool & the Gang, but he could not tell Paul McCartney from Pavarotti. Sanchez may even have thought that he and not Johnny Mercer had inspired his band's name. Everything Sanchez knew about music he had learned on the street; he therefore was unable to communicate intelligently with trained players and considered the deficiency to be theirs. Sanchez's ignorance of music theory meant that he could not be trusted to remember simple three-part harmony. No one had failed to notice that the only voice being fed into Sanchez's deafening vocal monitor was his own. He spent much of his time on stage watching televised sports, checking his e-mail, flirting with women on their way to the restroom, or playing with one hand while repairing his gear with the other. To fill the hours between gigs, Sanchez roamed Key West mowing lawns, fixing pool decks, or subbing at hot-dog stands before his red-eye Monday drive back to Miami.

Juan Bautista Sanchez's ancestry was Puerto Rican, but his long-suffering wife was African-American. So thoroughly had Sanchez assimilated black culture that he perceived racist behavior in whites the way a Holocaust survivor's grandson might declare that the cruciform Chevrolet logo was anti-Semitic. One evening on stage in Ike Ireton's presence Sanchez averred that the reason he disliked playing Van Morrison's songs was that the Irish soul singer had once made an ethnically offensive remark. Ike silently dismissed this ridiculous claim and refrained from suggesting that Sanchez might have been thinking of a Florida cracker named *Jim* Morrison. Sanchez of course had no more use for the Doors than for any other Caucasian assemblage.

What Juan Bautista Sanchez lacked in musical depth he made up for in cheerleading ability. He could keep a crowd dancing late into the evening, so long as the stage was turned over to him and the rest of the band was willing to play his forgettable one-chord songs. Sanchez's vulgar spoken commentary embarrassed everyone in the room except Kenny Schuster. This superficial excitement was precisely the antidote to Dave Mandarine's mere virtuosity that Schuster had been seeking—after all, no bandleader who has kept his gig for fifteen years can be expected to reinvent himself often enough to satisfy a club owner and a staff who know his songs inside and out.

When Sanchez buttonholed Schuster one evening and delivered his bullshit spiel, the proprietor was sold. A week later, the bass chair of the Dave Mandarine Band belonged to Sanchez.

In this case the term *chair* was to be taken literally. Unlike nearly all the world's bass guitarists, arthritic Juan Bautista Sanchez played in a seated position like someone performing folk songs in a coffeehouse. His sprawling, beat-up equipment looked like a garage sale, and Sanchez's overamplified voice and instrument could not disguise the fact that he appeared as if he were attending his mother's funeral. If asked he would have said that this demeanor expressed his distaste for his partners' repertoires, but he delivered his own inconsequential tunes with the same rote ennui.

This unfortunate turn of events coincided with Kenny Schuster's long-awaited acknowledgment that Dave's regular drummer was putting the patrons to sleep. With Sanchez's backing, Schuster approached Dave and "suggested" that Ike Ireton take over the drums. Dave's opinion on the matter was not sought, but he agreed that an ear-splitting, booty-slapping bass player and a versatile singing drummer might liven up the proceedings.

Ike Ireton welcomed the invitation, but there was just one small problem: in the decade it had taken Dave to see the light, Ike had accepted a better offer. For the past half dozen years, Gary Robertson had become the Keys' most popular singer-songwriter; his trop-rock recordings sold in huge numbers throughout the world and had won numerous awards. Aggressive marketing and an infectiously positive attitude had made Robertson the

Keys' leading musical ambassador and a serious player in the tourism industry's campaign to promote the Keys lifestyle. Robertson had assembled the best band south of the mainland and had tried more than once to recruit Ike Ireton, always when Ike was otherwise engaged. By the time Dave Mandarine finally came through, Ike had become quite comfortable playing fun music with a congenial band that worked major events for several times the money anyone else in the region could pay. Ike accepted Dave's belated offer on the condition that Ike be free to sub out for Robertson's gigs, which always were announced weeks or months in advance.

For two years Ike Ireton enjoyed the best of both worlds: a high-profile gig that any good musician might have been glad to accept, and a cozy, secure club residency where he could leave his secondary drum set parked on stage.

What for Ike Ireton was a streak of overdue financial success was for Dave Mandarine, Juan Bautista Sanchez, and Kenny Schuster a mixed blessing. Things were fine when Ike was available, which was most of the time: Gary Robertson's gigs took place only during tourist season and rarely occurred two weeks in a row. But when Ike was absent, the house band had to resort to the usual gang of competent, nonsinging drummers who knew only their respective bits of Dave and Sanchez's disparate repertoires.

More than once Juan Bautista Sanchez had mentioned to Ike Ireton, Dave Mandarine, and anyone else who would listen that Kenny Schuster had begged Sanchez to move his whole band down from Miami and displace Dave altogether. The implication was that Schuster and company were so tired of Dave's act that a nightly rerun of *Soul Train* seemed like an improvement. Sanchez claimed that he had rebuffed Schuster's appeals and that he would never do anything to damage his friendship with Dave. Sanchez and Ike Ireton certainly had musical and cultural differences, but Sanchez had acknowledged that Ike was the only local drummer who listened carefully enough to do his music justice. On the other hand, Ike brought far more to the bandstand than Sanchez wanted; everything he required of a human percussionist was available in an electronic drum machine. Sanchez saw that it was difficult to bully a player who knew a hundred times more about music than he did. There was no denying, furthermore, that Ike and Dave had more in common than either of them had with Sanchez and that both of them stood in the way of Sanchez's plan to replace boring white music with boring black music.

Finally one evening when Ike was off playing happy songs for real money with Gary Robertson, Kenny Schuster took Dave aside and "suggested" that Sanchez bring down just his young drummer, who juggled no schedule conflicts and who knew no better than to accept Sanchez's illiterate posturing as law. With that edict, the hijacking of the Dave Mandarine Band was complete.

Dave presented this news to his old buddy Ike Ireton on stage the next night, five minutes before the gig. Kenny Schuster had arranged to be elsewhere, and Sanchez spent the evening pretending Ike did not exist. Ike understood that Dave was stuck between a rock and a hard place and that the only way for Dave to keep his besotted residency was to become *Summer Wind featuring Dave Mandarine.* Ike assured Dave of his continued friendship, but he resolved to have nothing further to do with Juan Bautista Sanchez, Kenny Schuster, or Martha Gellhorn's Tavern. Ike had long before learned to avoid Schuster's other establishment, an overrated, roach-infested pizza joint on No Name Key that happened to be responsible for the worst case of indigestion Ike had ever suffered.

Many weeks later, Sanchez made a couple of lame attempts to reconnect with Ike via hypocritical postings on Facebook. These Ike blocked and reported as spam.

By the end of January 2014, Ike Ireton had heard nothing further from Dave Mandarine except for an IRS Form 1099 mailed from Dave's accountant. In the months following Ike's dismissal, various musicians and patrons had told him that his presence at Martha Gellhorn's was sorely missed. The musical writer received these well-meaning remarks with a circumspect smile. As Gellhorn's husband knew better than anyone, bad experiences make good stories.

Fed up with the Keys' endemic underachievement, Ike Ireton relocated to the Miami suburb of Coral Gables late in 2014 and accepted a part-time administrative position with the local musicians' union and an adjunct professorship teaching woodwinds at the University of Miami.

The typical UM student pursuing a classical career had formulated concrete goals in childhood and did not worry Ike. But whenever a young jazzer or rocker expressed any curiosity about Key West, Ike responded in Jesse Jackson fashion: "Key West is a place in which to retire, not to aspire." After the kid had absorbed this gem, Ike would conclude, "For what you want to do, there are precisely three music towns in this country: New York, Nashville, and L.A. Pick one of them, and don't look back."

HOPE, FOR NOW

I am confident that the pseudonym I have given this delightful girl is unnecessary. She was a prostitute.

Having lived as a teenager overseas, where in certain places prostitution is a sanctioned feature of the tourist trade, and having heeded ample warnings to avoid these possibly unhealthy women, I had never known any desire to go in and fuck a whore. Strolling through a typical red-light district, I would be struck mainly by the sadness of it all. They were so young, or so old, their brazen attire so shabby and pathetic, the men who heckled them so vile, I could never imagine using one of those poor wretches for exercise.

One day my girlfriend was telling me about a colleague of hers who recently had suffered several unsuccessful job interviews and, her self-esteem at low ebb, had applied at a massage parlor. This was the midseventies, when these places were popping up like hamburger joints in every strip mall. In my naïveté I assumed they were legitimate extensions of the previous decade's holistic discoveries. I was genuinely surprised when Tatiana told me her friend had been asked to masturbate her prospective employer. (She did not.)

A year or so after Tatiana and I broke up, I found my curiosity piqued about these mysterious dens. One day I stumbled across several pages of ads in the phone book. *Wow. To what extent are they legal?* My thriftiness balked at the thought of paying for a hand job—especially one I probably could perform better, or at least more sincerely, myself. I had to admit, though, that I was intrigued by the idea of submitting to a woman whom I did not know and would never see again, who did not care about me, who lived in this strange world of uncertainty. It was an adventure. *What the hell.* I drove a few miles to a shrouded set of rooms above a suburban health-food store.

Of course I felt cheap. It was not the discomfort of producing my shriveled penis for a female physician. It was not the silly, pseudo-Arabian atmosphere. It was the contempt in which I assumed these women held men. I was about to contribute to a girl's degradation while putting a few dollars toward her rent. How weak and selfish we are.

I looked around, walked up the stairs, and turned the corner. A tall, middle-aged man in a dark business suit was just leaving. I wanted to bolt. Each of us looked away as we passed. I went in.

The place was so dark it took a moment for my eyes to adjust. There was a little foyer, soft chairs arranged in a corner, the only light, red, emanating from a small table lamp. I was alone for many uncomfortable seconds. Finally the door to a tiny office opened, and a buxom young blonde in a T-shirt and cutoffs smiled at me. *What if I know one of these girls?* She asked me to take a seat, explaining that she would love to "be with" me but that she had the flu. I myself was beginning to feel sick. She was not exactly ugly, though, so I decided to assess my options. I could always go home like someone with some sense. I sat down, taking in the mounds of *Clockwork Orange* velour, hoping I could disappear into one of the rooms before any other men came in.

After a few minutes a pretty Hispanic girl about my age appeared. She was as voluptuous as her partner, dressed in a sheer white blouse, no bra, and very short black shorts. She was about as far off my beaten path as I could imagine. *It might be fun.* I followed her down the hall.

She opened a door and ushered me inside. She stood in the doorway and collected my fifteen dollars. "Just take off your clothes and relax, and I'll be right back."

Utterly strange. She was not going to stay and undress me as part of her ritual. It was like the doctor's office after all. But now I was committed. I undressed and folded my clothes over a chair; I stayed near them, theorizing that at any moment a chorus line of news cameras might burst through the door. I looked around.

The massage table was in the corner. The white sheet and pillowcase were clean. A little sink hung on the wall; beside it, a footstool was stacked with soft white hand towels. On a small dresser sat bottles of baby oil and talcum powder. I did not look in the drawers. The walls were as dark as those of the foyer. Behind me hung one of those awful velvet paintings; only instead of Elvis or Jesus, this one featured the big-breasted mama of some redneck's dreams. I laughed at myself. *I'm standing naked in a renovated cubicle that months ago was part of a real-estate office or a ballet school, perhaps being filmed by the FBI, preparing to be whacked off by this friendly Pan-American who surely has more valuable skills to offer society.* But there I was, and in a moment she would be there too. I touched myself.

When the girl returned I was standing beside the table, feeling suddenly ridiculous about my erection. She entered the room and smiled. At my cock. Our eyes never met, not then, not at any moment during our time in that room. I smiled back, uselessly. She motioned for me to get on the table. I lay up on my back. She told me to turn over. *Perhaps this won't be quite so superficial.* Slowly and gently she began to rub, knead, and stroke my neck, shoulders, and back, making her way, briefly but pleasantly, all the way down to my feet. She treated every part of me with equal attention. I began to feel at ease.

"OK, turn over," she said softly.

Once again, she started at my neck and worked her way down to my toes. She did not touch my genitals, which by now were completely relaxed. After this pass she stopped and looked at me. That is, at my cock.

"OK, do you want oil or powder?" she asked it. She turned and reached for a towel, folding it across my chest.

At first I did not understand her accent. "Just do whatever you want," I said, ludicrously. What she wanted, I am sure, was to run out of there and go home to her family.

She looked perplexed. She surveyed my package, crossed her right hand over her left, and touched me with all her fingertips. I got hard immediately. She smiled. Then she curled her right thumb and index finger around my stiff organ and, without removing her left hand from its feathery work, began to stroke me. She was not gripping the skin and moving it up and down like a teenager; she was traveling the length of my cock, passing completely over the tip and then back down to the base. I figured this was foreplay. I closed my eyes and tried to concentrate. Had she been Tatiana, her light stroking would have been a delightful variation on a theme. After a while I realized what she had asked me before.

"Um, maybe we could try some oil," I whispered. I was hesitant to criticize her technique, given the placement of her left hand.

She smiled and stopped. She reached for the bottle, snapped it open, and poured a small quantity of oil onto my erection. The light fragrance arrived at the same time her forefinger curled once more around me. I warmed considerably. Now her long, easy strokes made sense. She smiled.

"What's your name?" I asked. I assumed she would lie—perhaps she invented a new persona for each client— but I could not help wanting to connect with her, to personalize this odd experience.

"Hope." She smiled at my cock, tightening her finger a little.

"What a pretty name." I throbbed a little, and she smiled.

Does she use the one finger because it's less messy, or because it gets the job done faster? Both, of course, you idiot. I was amazed at how effective was that single digit, gliding slowly up and down the entire length of my shaft, offering no mercy to the purple crown. It was at once tranquil and hotly stimulating, and I enjoyed letting her control me.

I knew that technically Hope, or whatever her name was, owed me half an hour of her time. I understood also that she rightly would have preferred to get away with anything less. On a baser level, though, I was aware that what she was doing felt very good indeed, and I wanted it to last. *Her next client might be a violent creep.*

"Um," I began, my voice now pitched somewhat higher, "would you mind slowing down a little?"

To my surprise, she smiled and did just that, reducing her pace to a delicious hint of motion. I was beginning to like this girl. She smiled patiently, feeling my light throbs, knowing she could take me over the edge any time she wanted. She tightened her grip ever so slightly. I wanted to touch her, express myself to her, give something back to her. It was so strange, lying there, the only contact between us being her left fingertips and that glorious *OK* sign. I remembered that this was a business transaction; this and nothing more was what I had purchased. As a freelancer myself, I respected her terms. She was as unavailable to me as any woman on the street. Still, there she was, stroking my penis, something only people dear to my heart had ever done; it was difficult to see her as a paid servant. That sort of thinking is how prostitutes get rich in a hurry.

Hope smiled knowingly. "You may touch me if you like, on the legs," she whispered. She began stroking a little harder, and very slightly faster.

Now that I had her permission, I felt even less welcome. I nonetheless reached out and lightly caressed the backs of her thighs. She smiled and tightened her grip. It was wonderful torture.

"Please slow down," I pleaded. Hope smiled benevolently and did as requested.

After several blissful minutes of this, when my throbs and sighs told her that release was seconds away, Hope removed her left hand and slipped it under the towel that lay across my now heaving chest. She lightly stroked my nipples with the back of her hand, tightening her grip and speeding up. I had held her off as long as I could; now I was *with* her, giving in to her generosity and her need to be free. I resigned myself to her as to a pilot who gently guides a huge airliner down to a flawless landing. Together we raced. She squeezed me now, massaging every inch, increasing her speed as the runway loomed up and up. She cupped her hand under the towel and angled it.

"Oh! Hope!"

I threw my head back into the pillow as Hope smiled widely.

She continued her full stroking until my tip could no longer take the stimulation; she then slowed down as gradually, confining her motion to the shaft, squeezing me now and then. As we taxied toward the gate, my breathing returning to normal, beads of sweat running down behind my rushing ears, Hope's gentle smile remained. When finally my throbbing subsided, she made one or two more passes and shut down the engines, petting my still-hard penis with what I dearly wanted to interpret as affection.

She gathered up her towel, folded it neatly, and set it down on the table. She picked up a fresh towel and laid it gently across my sizzling member. Then she turned to the sink and ran warm water.

"Oh, God. That was beautiful. Thank you, Hope." I felt bonded with her. Whatever difficulties had led her to this work, she was good at it.

"You're welcome. Now, just relax."

Hope turned back to me and wiped away most of the oil, as tenderly as a lover, all the while smiling with contentment, or relief. "How do you feel?" she whispered.

"Wonderful."

"Good. It was nice to meet you."

Hope patted me a few times, folded the second towel, retrieved the first, and walked to the door. Opening it, she looked back and smiled. At my cock. Then she disappeared, her high heels clicking into the distance.

I lay there a moment. Alone again in that sad room, without Hope's circumspect humanity, with only the pleasant aftermath of my orgasm and the garish velvet tits on the wall, I felt the emptiness again. A whore and her lonely john. I knew this was just my male chemistry taking over, that my attitude would be completely different if she were a girlfriend, lying at my side, twirling her fingers through my chest hair, listening to the heartbeat she had set to soaring. But it was what it was, and I had to get out of there. I got off the table, the floor now cold against my bare feet. I dressed quickly, took one more bemused look around, and left.

Halfway down the hall I met Hope coming my way. She was alone.

She smiled and quite professionally offered her hand.

"Thank you again," I said. "Take care."

Finally our eyes met.

"I will. Goodnight."

"Goodnight."

In later years, during similar periods of isolation, I would visit several other sensual masseuses; the thrill of a stranger's touch was too alluring not to sample now and then. Those girls proved Hope to have been a neatnik after all: they lavished me with oil and used every part of both hands and watched with palpable excitement; they saved towels, the first soaked in warm aromatic water, for the closing minutes of our encounter. Some of these beauties bathed me head to toe, before or after the massage. I learned to enjoy these visits on their own terms, but I never left without wishing the girl had asked me to return her favor.

THE IMPRESARIO

Fuck.

Monroe County homicide detective Rich Castillo put down the phone and stared out at the coconut palm swaying too close to his office window. He had just received word that his partner, Sergeant Alvin Varela, had been shot in the right leg the previous night in a Stock Island convenience store.

Varela was off duty at the time and accidentally interrupted an attempted holdup. He managed to kick the gun out of a desperate robber's hand and, with the proprietor's help, restrained the teenage crackhead until backup arrived. The minor hero was now lying in a bed at Lower Keys Medical Center and was expected to be off the street—and off the salsa dance floor at El Meson de Pepe— for eight weeks.

As Castillo prepared to walk the short distance to the hospital to visit his friend, he lamented two sudden realities and could not decide which was worse: (1) the detective would temporarily be saddled with a new, probably younger and less compatible partner, and (2) the Rich Castillo Band, in which Alvin Varela played percolating bass alongside Castillo's irresistible drumming, would have to cancel two months' gigs. Unlike most Key West bands, Castillo's outfit played mostly original music and, since that music featured exquisite four-part harmonies and thoughtful arrangements, actually rehearsed. Castillo would not even consider hiring

61

someone to sub for one half of the Keys' premier rhythm section. The loss of moonlighting income was hardly a disaster for Castillo, given that local club owners knew they could get away with paying their nonunion entertainers nineteen sixties wages; but the absence of Varela's companionship and of all four band members' main creative outlet was a bummer. Castillo dreaded delivering the news to guitarists Ed Carlyle and Vladimir "Velvet" Voznesensky, but it was too early in the day to call them—unlike Castillo and Varela, the two freelancers had no day job to fill in the musical gaps—and the drummer wanted to be able to tell them more about Varela's condition.

Having confirmed that his partner was not permanently injured and was in typically good spirits, Castillo returned to his office to call the other two and to consider his immediate future.

Rich Castillo kept up his chops with regular workouts on a set of rubberized wood practice pads that his neighbors on narrow Poorhouse Lane could not hear, but earnest repetition in a ticking studio was no substitute for the quick reflexes needed in the charged atmosphere of the gig. After a history of declining offers from Key West's assortment of lackluster musicians, the University of Miami alum decided to throw caution to the wind. It did not take long for word to get out that the respected drummer was temporarily available and for his cell phone to begin ringing at rude hours.

As he had expected, Lieutenant Rich Castillo was handed an interim partner straight out of the academy. The county sheriff and his wife, friends of the kid's widowed mom, prevailed on Castillo to take him on as a personal favor. When after a few rides together Castillo reported that the kid had uttered the most offensive racist and xenophobic language he had ever heard, the sheriff reassigned the rookie to guard detail at the little county airport: the departmental purgatory for problem children. The remainder of Alvin Varela's convalescence was filled with another new recruit whose only drawback was her stunning Mediterranean beauty. Castillo even noticed a disturbing resemblance to his girlfriend, massage therapist Victoria Landini—an observation Castillo wisely kept to himself.

The first of Castillo's sometime freelance music clients to buttonhole him was the mountainous and entertaining bluesman Elliott "Grizzly" Clatterbuck, who, following years of shuttling between Key West and his native Atlanta, had secured himself a house gig at a renovated former jazz club at the corner of Front and Whitehead Streets. El Fumadero Cubano occupied the floor above the owner's cigar shop and offered a menu of stale air, bland food, and live blues six nights a week. Clatterbuck's regular drummer was a loudmouthed drunk who kept his gig solely by providing the P.A. system that broadcast the club's uninvited repertoire to the cruise-ship passengers disembarking across the street at Mallory Square, and Griz was eager to capitalize on any opportunity to offer his listeners a bit of variety in addition to steady timekeeping.

Castillo had enjoyed playing with Clatterbuck sporadically over the years and slipped back into the bassist's old-school driver's seat as if he had never left. It was actually a relief just to sit back and groove without thinking about intricate vocal parts and the many other details of leading his own band. Castillo hated playing the student-quality house drum set, soiled as it was by dust, cigar ashes, sticky cocktail stains, and drumstick shavings, but its presence made the amateurish situation that much easier to walk away from when the night was over.

Less tolerable was the behavior of the omnipresent club owner, Nicky Molinari. The tall, pale, muscular man of no discernible hair color paced through the room a hundred times a night between trips downstairs to check on the cigar store. Molinari sported a uniform of sorts, consisting of brown alligator cowboy boots, tight blue jeans, any of several tight dark Harley-Davidson T-shirts, and any of several nonmatching paisley bandannas worn as head scarves. Patrons often mistook the proprietor for a busboy or for one of their own, and Molinari did not seem bothered by their reaction to his ludicrous appearance. When Molinari addressed the musicians it generally was with a stream of snarling negativity regarding their volume—always too loud or too soft, despite unchanged settings—or their curious habit of expecting to be treated as human beings when approaching the bar during a break. Molinari thought nothing of ascending the stage in the middle of a song and taking over the mixing board to ensure that defenseless pedestrians on the sidewalks below were gaining the full benefit of his musical ignorance. Equally amusing was Molinari's penchant for calling individual musicians *brother,* as if they had something in common besides the perilous economy.

Financially, Nicky Molinari was the worst offender among Key West's notoriously cheap club owners. To afford six weekly nights of live music featuring not just typical guitar trios but full five- and six-piece bands with keyboards and horns, Molinari paid rock-bottom money to the dregs of the local scene. Grizzly Clatterbuck, who suffered various health problems and who a few years before had been effectively homeless, had rushed to accept his steady weekend gig despite the insulting pay; he was considered the club's headliner. The other three nights brought in musicians who would have been hard pressed to find professional employment of any kind in a real city. They did not complain about the bread because they knew even less about the business than they did about their craft.

On a break one evening after enduring the lesbian bartender's routinely surly reception, Castillo walked outside to breathe some fresh air. He went down the steps to the street, where he encountered Molinari milling about in front of his deserted shop. The club owner kept in constant cell-phone contact with his upstairs staff, who shared his opinion that the musicians who kept his business open were at best unwelcome visitors. Sensing Castillo's discomfort, Molinari sidled over to him and asked if everything was all right.

Years of bandleading had taught Rich Castillo to interact with club owners only when absolutely necessary. But his itinerant relationship with Molinari, who struck him as just the latest in a long line of arrogant fools hoping to make a killing exploiting Key West's clueless tourists, inspired the drummer to make an exception. He did not expect the conversation to go well, and it did not.

"You might want to offer your bartender a brief lesson

in etiquette," Castillo smiled.

"Oh?" Molinari replied. "How's that, brother?"

Castillo described the treatment he had just received, which both men knew was typical.

"Well, my customers come first," Molinari said defensively.

"Yes," Castillo answered, estimating that he had been performing in nightclubs when his inquisitor was still sucking his thumb, "but the room is practically empty, and, as usual, Corrine went out of her way to avoid me as if she actually had something to do."

"Maybe she did."

"She was standing around talking with a girlfriend and ignoring customers besides myself."

"You're not my customer. You're my employee."

"Nonsense," Castillo replied. "I am an independent contractor, like the guy who delivered this now lukewarm Heineken. You pay us in cash, off the books, from what I hear, and you don't contribute to our health care or pension. That's not an employer-employee relationship."

Molinari stepped back and smiled. "You know, brother, I'm pretty generous with you guys."

Castillo suppressed a laugh.

"You get a free meal and two free drinks a night. That could stop."

"We wish it would," Castillo countered. "In exchange for your lousy food, your slow service, and the same beer we have at home, we'd prefer a living wage."

Molinari, who knew nothing of Castillo's day job, drew himself fully upright. "Have you ever owned a restaurant?" he asked.

"Of course not," Castillo replied. "Have you?"

"Look, pal, I don't think I like your tone."

Castillo chuckled. "Well, if your drummer knew anything about tuning, maybe his crappy instruments would resonate more to your liking."

Failing to get the joke, Molinari edged forward.

The Miami native stood his ground. "Do you have any idea what musicians earn in the real world? You cannot continue treating us as second-class citizens."

A long silence ensued.

Finally Molinari answered, "Well, that's your perception. Everyone else who plays here seems perfectly happy to do so."

"Actually," Castillo replied, "that's not quite the case. First of all, I'm here tonight only as a favor to an old acquaintance. Second, I wouldn't hire any of those hacks upstairs to play a backyard barbeque. And third, I know for a fact that every musician who's ever played here thinks you're a complete asshole. Next question?"

Molinari seemed on the verge of employing his impressive musculature. "You know, I don't think this is working out."

Castillo laughed. "Oh, you noticed that? Well, at least we agree on something, albeit for different reasons. But as I said, you can't fire someone who doesn't work for you."

"OK, pal," Molinari exhaled inches from Castillo's face, "when this next set is over you can take your drums and get the fuck out of here."

Smiling politely, Castillo answered, "Well, once again, I wouldn't own that drum set if you were giving it away. But you may be certain that I have no further need for your company." Castillo poured his unfinished beer into the gutter, tossed the bottle into a recycling bin, and walked back upstairs.

At the end of the night, the band as usual had to wait nearly an hour to get paid. Castillo pocketed his chump change, grabbed his stick bag, and headed for the door.

Molinari was awaiting Castillo on the landing. "We need to talk," he said with authority.

"No, we don't," Castillo smiled as he headed down the steps.

"Don't walk away from me, pal," Molinari said.

Castillo stopped, turned, and considered his options. A simple display of his badge probably would silence Molinari for good: it was widely known that the businessman owed money to vendors all over town, including the sign painter who had eradicated all wistful traces of the defunct jazz club. And of course Castillo never went anywhere without a firearm. His fatigue, from the gig and from Molinari's tedious existence, was another factor. But the idiot was offering a fun epilogue to an otherwise worthless evening. "Look, man, I didn't ask to be here, and I definitely won't be back. But let me give you a piece of advice."

Molinari gripped the banister.

Castillo continued: "A year from now, when you're sitting in bankruptcy court, dressed, I would recommend, not as Willie Nelson's bus driver but rather as someone who might expect to be taken seriously, maybe you'll consider finding yourself an honorable way to make a living. Playing impresario, that is, ripping off educated musicians doesn't seem to be your calling."

Molinari made a move toward Castillo.

"And unless you'd like to add a few criminal charges into the mix," the cop said while reaching under his shirttail, "I suggest you keep your hands to yourself."

Molinari stood trembling with clenched fists. "Fuck you!" he screamed.

Castillo laughed. "Exactly." He turned, descended the stairs, crossed the street, and got in his minivan. He lowered the windows and sat a while in the sea breeze, letting the embarrassing night sink in. The musician had never allowed one of these clowns to bait him, and he swore to himself that it would not happen again. He started the engine and drove home.

Nine months later El Fumadero Cubano went out of business, but the touristy smoke shop remained open. Nicky Molinari contented himself with the commerce of day-trippers whose fantasies convinced them that buying a thirty-dollar cigar a hundred yards from their waiting cruise ship, having seen nothing of the real Key West, would somehow imbue them with the mystique left lingering in the jasmine air by the town's long-dead literary heroes. When news of Molinari's fiscal dealings became public—it turned out that, like many of his colleagues, the club owner had supported his own fantasy with a thriving sideline in pharmaceutical sales—no one bothered to say *I told you so.*

Nicky Molinari turned up dead from blunt trauma late one night in the alley behind the Red Garter strip club. Rich Castillo and Alvin Varela got the call. As they awaited the forensic team to make sense of Molinari's multiple injuries, the two cops agreed that the perpetrator could have been anyone from the sign painter to the guy who used to deliver the Heineken. They ruled out most of their fellow musicians, simply because people in that profession tend to be unfit pacifists. By dawn the murder weapon was determined to have been a heavy, probably wooden object such as a baseball bat.

The next time Rich Castillo heard from Elliott "Grizzly" Clatterbuck, it was via a Facebook posting announcing the bluesman's new residency at a popular nightspot in Tokyo. Neither Castillo nor Varela, who was equally particular about the quality of his instruments, would have had any reason to know that Clatterbuck's bastardized Fender bass guitar had recently been thoroughly cleaned up and was now available for purchase on eBay.

JOCELYN DAVIES

Jocelyn Davies worked in a pop duo with a former boyfriend, Joel Feinstein. She also shared an apartment with him. They decided to add a third musician and found me. We were all in our midtwenties.

She had an earthy, friendly face, short dust-blonde hair, a vivacious personality, and an irresistible smile. She also had a great ass. It was her most striking feature. Small, tight, perfectly round, begging to be touched. She had ample, shapely breasts and an attractive, trim figure all around, but it was that cute butt that caught my eye. She later said that what turned her on about me was the way I took care of my instruments. I thought, *Why do women always have to show off their damned integrity?*

Despite noticing each other from the start, Jocelyn and I maintained a cheerfully platonic relationship for months. Even though she and Joel had long before stopped having sex, neither was seeing anyone else; the mere fact that they still lived together was intimidating. I genuinely cared for them both.

As Jocelyn and I became closer, she began to admit to me that their arrangement was unnatural—they had only briefly been intimate—and that each of them was just waiting for the courage or the motivation to move out. I interpreted this confession not as a green light but simply as a friend's uncertainty shared. She and her partner had too much history.

Over time Jocelyn confided in me more, and we addressed all the topics of the day and of our lives. After a rehearsal or a meeting, Joel would pad off to bed and Jocelyn and I would share the sofa talking late into the night. Our personal bond was deepening, but there still was no overt sexual charge.

Then one night, as I rose to leave, we found ourselves positioned a little closer than usual. Something new was in the air. We did not make eye contact. Suddenly we embraced. It felt like incest. Jocelyn was shaking.

"My God, what is happening?" she whispered into my collar.

I held her softly.

"I'm scared," she said.

"It's all right," I replied, stroking her hair.

We stayed in each other's arms a long time, afraid to face each other, afraid to jump from a runaway train. Had we been in denial? If we went forward, would it open an old wound? Would Joel resent her for being the one to break the stalemate? Would their partnership survive? And, having slipped into this dimension, how could Jocelyn and I pretend it did not exist? In doing the right thing, would not we just prolong their strange monasticism and deprive all three of us of love and freedom? Such confusion from one little hug.

Jocelyn wept softly. There was more than physical or emotional need in her tightening embrace. She wanted not only to be loved, but to be rescued. I stroked the small of her back.

Jocelyn began to relax. She patted my shoulders. Maybe she was coming to her senses. She kissed my cheek.

I kissed hers, savoring her warm breath on my neck. Still not having faced each other, we held on, not knowing what to say. Then, simultaneously, we pulled around and kissed each other hard on the mouth.

"Oh, God," Jocelyn shuddered, as her hands began to explore me.

I held onto her in silence. It had been a wonderful kiss, her full, rich lips passionate and seeking, her shy tongue leaving little doubt. Her back was moist.

"What are we going to do?" she asked.

"Let's just sleep on it."

We were terrified that Joel had been lying in the next room, awake, noticing the odd silence.

I took Jocelyn's athletic shoulders in my hands and looked at her. She smiled, averting her eyes. I put my arm around her and walked her to the door, touched her chin, and kissed her lightly. "Don't worry." I walked a few steps into the hallway and turned.

She was standing in the doorway, smiling brightly. At first she looked like good old Jocelyn with the dynamic stage presence. But my friend looked me up and down like a lover.

I went home and wrote a song about her, one of my best. When next we laid eyes on each other, a few days later, it was clear we were in love.

Our evening talk became a hushed kissing and petting session. We were ever mindful of Joel's presence, the increasingly late hour, the need to break away. My place was out of the question because my roommates still considered the duo a couple. I complimented her touch.

"It's so easy," she whispered, gliding her palm over my

bulge, outlining the shape with long, beautiful fingers.

One night Jocelyn was overcome with desire and unsnapped my jeans. The little click resonated like a geological fissure. We paused and listened. Then, grinning like a naughty child, she slowly lowered my zipper. My hardness moved forward. We kissed, and Jocelyn slipped her hand inside. For several minutes we suffered our maddening suspense.

Jocelyn pushed me back against the sofa and tugged at my jeans, lowering them just enough to have access. She moaned softly as she slipped my boxers down. We tried to stay alert. After a few minutes she took me in her mouth. Then she withdrew. "I want you *inside* me," she whispered urgently. She began to masturbate me.

She felt wonderful, but I could not relax. Joel was inches away on the other side of the wall, there was little I could do for Jocelyn in this setting, and at any rate she was just too eager. I gently pulled on her shoulder. She looked hurt.

"I'm sorry," I whispered. "We need to find a place."

Jocelyn smiled and embraced me. Reluctantly I pulled up my pants. We sat back and admitted we were getting reckless.

The next night, though, she was on me again, working repetitiously as on a difficult melody, trying to milk some release from our repressive situation. I stroked her lovely ass through her jeans, wishing I could quiet my brain and give Jocelyn the prize she so impatiently sought. But there was something more. Besides trying too hard, she did not have the rhythm. She was like a teenager willing to do any clumsy thing to keep her boyfriend.

This sad crusade continued for a few nights. Eventually Jocelyn began to feel dejected. I consoled her and promised that our lovemaking would blossom in the right environment. But she was determined to make me come, and she saw her fruitless labor as a sign of inadequacy.

Part of Jocelyn's resolve lay in the fact that she just really loved my cock, as an object. She loved to touch it, kiss it, look at it. Without any preliminaries she would open my pants and bring me joyfully to a full yearning erection, then sit back and admire her trophy. "It's so pretty," she would say with childlike wonder, petting it as she would a kitten.

Finally one spring weekend Joel went out of town. Jocelyn met me at her door framed in brilliant morning sun, beaming with anticipation. She lived on the water, several stories up, and the sparkling view refreshed us. We opened all the windows, had breakfast, and went to her bed.

As luck would have it, Jocelyn was on her period; we made a spectacular mess. It was a funny postscript to our long frustration. But nothing, probably not even the possibility of Joel's walking through the door, could have kept us apart that morning. We made love all day. We were so primed for the main event that we had only intercourse, over and over, until we collapsed in giddy exhaustion. Each of us luxuriated in fully satisfying climaxes. As the evening sun began to recline, we showered and took a slow walk in the grass at the river's edge. We held hands, feeling mated, drained, reborn.

We began the delicate choreography of schedules and

opportunities, rooms and cars, stolen looks and wiped smiles. We wanted just to tell Joel and get it out in the open. For weeks he either did not see or refused to acknowledge what was happening before his eyes. Finally, as Jocelyn was arranging a long trip to visit her family, it came out accidentally that I was going with her. It was not the way we had hoped to break the news.

Joel then admitted he had felt our developing relationship but had decided not to interfere. It stung, he confessed, but he understood that this had been inevitable, necessary. His brotherly love for his singer and his friendship for me remained undiminished. He also would have the last laugh: a few years later he married a gorgeous brunette who could have stepped out of my wildest fantasies. I miss him.

On our journey to her parents', Jocelyn and I were so ravenous for each other, and so acutely aware that our activities in the family house would be even more restricted than in her apartment, that we pulled off the highway several times to make love.

On one of those occasions we discovered a phenomenon that would bless our union with happy frequency: simultaneous orgasm. Experiencing Jocelyn's breathing, motions, and sounds rising in tandem with my own, sharing the glorious eruption rocking through us at exactly the same time, one body, one mind, one soul, in perfect harmony with the universe, defined the word *alive*. Knowing that that potential was within us was pure power, and excellent reinforcement for Jocelyn's fragile ego.

Jocelyn still had one mountain to climb, though, and she remained determined to conquer it. Despite several attempts she still had not been able to masturbate me to completion, even using her mouth and both hands. Having tried all the gentle encouragement I knew, finally I realized that a little demonstration was in order. It could not insult Jocelyn nearly so much as she was punishing herself.

We were in her parents' living room one night after everyone else had gone to bed. I was sitting on the sofa, and Jocelyn was leaning over me, doing her best, both of us haunted not only by our poor track record but also by the need to remain absolutely quiet. I lay back and concentrated to no avail. It was beginning to get funny. It already felt like a jinx. From the standpoint of my pleading cock, it was becoming a real drag. I tapped lightly on Jocelyn's back. She was about to burst into tears.

I held her tenderly while my red-faced, bewildered soldier stood patiently at attention. Silently I reminded myself of our outstanding intercourse.

"I love you so much," I whispered. "Just put your lips on me, at the tip, and I'll do the rest."

Jocelyn smiled and nodded. She was willing to try anything. And the thought of my jacking off into her mouth turned her on more than she was showing.

Only one other woman, during college, had ever persuaded me to masturbate for her, and that was simply because she wanted to watch; technique was not among that girl's many other problems.

More adult student than scholastic enabler, Jocelyn leaned down and placed her lips on me. I gave her ample opportunity to feel my pacing.

"Mmmm," she registered several minutes later.

"Mm-hmm," I answered, massaging her neck as my

tide rushed in.

She moaned softly and caressed me everywhere, swallowing quietly as my orgasm resolved. When finally I removed my hand, she took the whole thing in her mouth and made several hungry passes before sitting up. She wore a new smile.

"Wow. It's hot. Not warm. *Hot.* I've never done that before!"

There were other wonderful things Jocelyn had never done before, as it turned out. How exciting it was to enter her from behind, reassuring her; how thrilling to give her my tongue, teasing her nipples with wet fingertips while she sighed musically. And how happy for her I was when finally one afternoon in her own bed she lay down beside me, took me in her mouth, and quietly stroked me to a long, deep climax. Left-handed.

KARLA IN THE CLOSET

From a journal found in the storage room backstage at the Green Parrot Bar, Key West

The lesbian reader expecting a tale of melting denial will perhaps be disappointed to learn that this story involves an actual closet. The author suggests that such a reader's curiosity will nonetheless have its rewards.

Karla Saladin was a dark beauty; her ancestry was Syrian. Raven hair blessed her shoulders like sacred cloth; deep brown eyes penetrated me from a bronze portrait of nobility. From her strong jaw to the eminently kissable tip of her slender nose, she was breathtaking. She had the compact frame of a gymnast. Just looking at Karla made my pussy wet, but I already had learned that it did not take much for that to happen.

We met at our community swim club on Long Island in 1966. She was entering the eighth grade, I the ninth. I would admire her gliding along the water's edge before diving gracefully, but her body was not the focus of my wonder so much as her elegant face and her sheer poise.

Karla had grown up with a domineering father who lavished attention on her older brother, a promising baseball player. She was shy in matters of romance and had never gone beyond kissing. Every fragile bridge we crossed was a lesson in gentleness. We probably would never have entered into a sexual relationship had we not fallen so deeply in love.

I was amazed the first time I saw Karla's breasts. They were of average size for her thirteen years, but the areolas and nipples were ripe and womanly. I loved to kiss them.

It was months before Karla allowed me to touch her vagina, outside her clothes, and weeks more before her anxiety subsided enough to let my hand venture under her swimsuit.

We were in the woods behind the pool, lying in a little clearing. Karla arched her back sharply when I slipped my finger just a bit inside her. I assumed it was in pleasure. But when I looked at her face, I saw she was fighting back tears.

"It hurts," she said, apologetically.

Gently I removed my hand and embraced her. "I'll never hurt you again."

Karla often babysat for her neighbors. It was on these occasions, quietly negotiating a stranger's couch after the children were asleep, that we made our early discoveries, taking our time.

One such evening I actually persuaded Karla to take off her panties. She was lovely. Gradually I made my way down and tended to her. She was too uncomfortable to enjoy it much, and we laughed at seeing each other from this new perspective.

Karla had touched me outside my pants but had not seen me. It was with a feeling of liberation that I lowered my jeans for her. I was lying on my back on the sofa; Karla knelt beside me on the rug. With tender fascination she began to stroke and caress me. She was of course more surprised than I at my abundant moisture.

Having so easily gone down on Karla, I began to fantasize about how wonderful her mouth would feel on me. We joked about it more than once before she got up her courage.

The first time was more comic than erotic. She was babysitting in the late afternoon, and the mother was due home any minute. I rose to leave. At the door I turned to kiss Karla goodbye. When we embraced she pressed herself warmly against me.

I undid my pants. "Please. Just for a second, and I'll go."

"No! You've got to get out of here!"

We both were laughing, but my pussy was dead serious. I would never have forced it on her, of course, and the whole episode lasted less than a minute. But since I was blocking the door, Karla figured there was only one way to get rid of me. She looked down, started to laugh again, and then, quite unexpectedly, became quiet and composed. She leaned over, causing her long, silken hair to fall forward. As she pulled it aside I was struck with her magnificent beauty. In the next instant she knelt and gave me one long stroke of her tongue, finished with the briefest of kisses. Shocking warmth filled me. Just as quickly, she drew back and stood.

"Oh!" I cried, as immediately we resumed laughing.

"Now, go!" she commanded.

I pulled up my pants and kissed Karla again. She tasted of the sea. "Thank you. I love you." Leaving, I took in one last gaze; her infinite eyes confirmed that we had awakened an irresistible new thrill.

Although Karla had no trouble arousing me, her own responses were always less pronounced. I longed to help her loosen up. I always felt that my pleasure surpassed hers.

Karla tried to masturbate me several times, and she was always glad to give me her mouth. Our mutual inexperience, compounded, I am sure, by the guilty environments in which we met, prevented our coming. It hardly mattered.

Early in the summer of 1967 my parents left town for two weeks, leaving me, a fifteen-year-old, in charge of the house. Because of nerves and schedules—I was in summer school to atone for failing algebra—Karla and I did not take advantage of this opportunity until a few days before Mom and Dad were due back.

Thinking of alert neighbors, Karla slipped in the kitchen door on that balmy morning. I had just emerged from the shower and, in anticipation, had not dressed. Having never seen me nude, Karla was a bit startled; but she warmed up when I held her in my arms. Through her soft T-shirt I could feel the moisture of her anxiety. We went to my room.

Slowly I undressed her. So beautiful. Holding her this way, our warm, naked bodies pressed together, was like a dream.

We lay on my bed for a while, kissing and touching, enveloped in youthful excitement.

Out of nowhere, Karla said, "Wouldn't it be funny if your parents came home early?"

We both giggled.

As a joke, I straightened up and peeked through my closed blinds—*and there they were, pulling in the driveway!*

We panicked.

"Quick! Get in the closet!" I exclaimed, jumping into my jeans. "They have no reason to come in here. I'll think of something."

Karla gathered up her clothes, turned to me in terror, which I tried briefly to assuage, and, still nude, disappeared into my closet. Once inside she was quiet as a mouse. I could have told her how wonderful she was, how someday we would laugh about this. Instead I took a deep breath, closed my bedroom door behind me, and went out to greet my folks.

They set about unpacking the car, giving me time. I did not yet dare try to sneak Karla out; too many trips were being made up and down the hall.

Then I had a brainstorm. I called an older friend who had a car and asked her to come over. The idea was to make it look as if she had brought Karla with her. The only difficulty would be in making sure she arrived at a moment when I could whisk Karla out of the closet and into the living room when Mom and Dad were otherwise occupied so it would appear the two had arrived together.

It worked. My friend arrived precisely when no one was upstairs, I dashed in and retrieved my trembling girlfriend, and the three of us assembled on the sofa. By the time my parents breezed by, everything looked perfectly normal.

Well, almost everything.

As we were sitting there congratulating ourselves, I

placed my hand on Karla's back to savor our little victory. I patted her softly on the pocket.

Fortunately no one noticed that either, and a quick trip to the bathroom set all the planets back in their assigned orbits.

Several weeks later my folks told me Dad had been appointed to a foreign diplomatic post. I had one month in which to bid farewell to everyone and everything I knew.

Karla and I corresponded constantly, pouring out our agonized love. We vowed to remain true. We kept that vow for the better part of the fall semester, until I succumbed to temptation and she to a social scene that required a decorative boyfriend. Adolescent jealousy and the delights of a sexy new girl prevented my fighting for Karla. In our hearts, though, both of us knew that we were number one and that our day might come again.

Years afterward I learned that the reason my parents had gone away and entrusted their home to me was not simply to vacation before going overseas but rather to repair their relationship after Mom discovered Dad was having an affair with his secretary. That the brief getaway was unsuccessful explained their surprising reappearance.

On my return to the States, Karla and I renewed our affections, cooled somewhat by our own other alliances. We stayed in touch and enjoyed the odd moment of guilty reunion.

Another year passed. One day in 1971 the phone rang in my dorm room. Karla had enrolled at the same college.

Once again, our timing was off. She was still seeing the guy back home who followed me. I was juggling two or three liaisons, sometimes not too gracefully. But Karla was important. The next year, as I was between relationships and she was bored with hers, we began dating again.

I had moved off campus into a great little apartment above a garage. One night after the theater, Karla told her roommate not to wait up.

It was wonderful to welcome Karla to my bed, again to feel the fullness of her warm, naked body—and we did not have to worry about my parents' driving up. We kissed and touched each other for a long time, her heat unguarded for the first time as I trembled against her side. She was still a virgin in the traditional sense, and I had no intention of changing that without her explicit permission. I still could not shake the feeling that I had less to offer than she. Karla was there to perform a sacrifice. She reached over to my nightstand and ran her fingers up and down the long, thick dildo I kept there.

"Are you sure, Karla?" I asked.

"Yes."

I was not convinced, nor did I doubt that this consummation meant everything to her. I reached into the drawer, pulled out my leather harness, fed the cock through the ring, and looked into Karla's eyes. "You're sure."

"Yes. Please. Make love to me."

I strapped the thing on, half expecting my virgin to spoil the mood with nervous laughter, and positioned myself above Karla. I kissed her as I reached down. I introduced the tip, slowly, remembering the pain my finger had caused her that day behind the pool. Karla gasped and arched her back, exactly as before. Her heart was so out of sync with the rest of her body.

"It's OK," she whispered.

"We need to relax."

Supporting myself with my elbows, I stroked her dark eyebrows, the perfect line of her cheekbones, her olive neck, shoulders, and breasts, all the while keeping the tip just inside her. I kissed her everywhere I could reach. Eventually, when I felt her tension subside, I eased it a bit farther in, stopping at the twitch of her spine. After many minutes like this I managed to get it in about halfway and began moving slowly. Karla pretended to enjoy it.

"We don't have to do this now, you know."

"No. I want you inside me."

The thing felt like a weapon, giving no pleasure as every little motion made Karla wince.

"Please. Love me."

I concentrated on her beautiful face, covering her with kisses, as I resumed my light movement. She would contract every time I tried to go a little farther in. After a while she started to smooth out. Her breathing was lovely, the sweat on her brow beginning to run down her temples.

All this time Karla had not raised her thighs off the bed, and I had not sought to do it for her. Suddenly she relaxed a bit and widened her legs, just as I was entering her, causing the toy to go in all the way for the first time. Karla screamed, and I stopped. Slowly I withdrew to my previous position and comforted her. After a few moments I gradually resumed subtle movements.

"How can I make you love me?" she sobbed.

"Karla, you know I do." I was fucking an angel, hurting her, but she would not let me stop. She was crying, pulling me in. I wanted this to be over.

I reached back and took her right hand, which was clenched into a fist. Gently I pried open her fingers and placed the hand between my legs. Her pleasing me might counteract my abusing her.

Finally she was enjoying my movements. She held me so tightly with her free arm that my efforts on her behalf became work. At the same time, what she was doing with her other hand was about to make me come.

I managed to keep the cock halfway outside her as my body shook. "Oh! Karla!"

As my orgasm subsided, we lay quietly for a while, stroking each other's hair, tracing sweat with our fingertips. Karla's hands on my back, open and at ease, were once again the agents of joy I had known before our terrible dance.

"God, that hurt so good," she laughed, as I eased down next to her. "Can we do it again?"

I looked at her. "Let's wait a little while."

We did not use the toy again that night, though we probably should have. Instead we lay in each other's arms, kissed, and drifted off to sleep.

The next morning I woke to find Karla lying beside me with her head on my chest. She was caressing me lightly. As she began to realize I was awake, her circular motion became more earnest.

"Is this what you want?" I whispered.

"Yes. Come for me."

I lay my head back and gave myself over to her.

Our first attempt at penetration might have been our last. Timing continued to plague us. We saw each other now and again, nonsexually. But I met someone, and Karla eventually married the guy back home. It was a mistake. The jerk left her when their daughter was born, six weeks premature.

Karla moved to D.C., worked for the federal government, found a second boyfriend, and gave her life to her fragile child. We had dinner together in New York in 1990; her eyes still had their power over me. Much had changed. But whenever we met or spoke on the phone, the undeniable vibration of love was there. Neither of us expected the stunning second reunion that was to come.

Karla and I used the annual winter holiday card as an excuse to let each other know that our unresolved love was still alive. But her 1994 message was so urgent and so beautifully written that her physical reappearance felt inevitable. Karla had married the boyfriend to give her daughter a father figure and had accepted the resultant complacency. Her girl, now eleven, required less supervision. Karla's restlessness had swelled to meet her hunger.

I called Karla the day after receiving her card and asked if she would mind picking me up at National Airport. She burst into tears of joy. A connoisseur of choral music, Karla welcomed my belated gift: two tickets to a performance of Bach's *Christmas Oratorio* at the Kennedy Center.

I had to rely on vestiges of music-appreciation class to get through the concert sitting next to fantastic Karla. When I would look into those intense dark eyes, so full of memories informed by a woman's wisdom, I nearly fainted. Afterward, we went to her car and drove to my hotel.

Kissing Karla's supple lips after so long was luscious. I could have spent the night just touching her black hair and the milk-chocolate back of her neck. Karla had grown fabulously orgasmic, able to come quickly and in a variety of ways. When fully aroused, her unusually large clit showed itself as the incipient penis that might have been if not for Lady Luck. As before, Karla's patience commanded me to enjoy her tongue for nearly an hour before introducing my expanded collection of toys. (Airport security in those days was not quite so intrusive as it is today.) I was honored finally to know Karla this way.

Ultimately, once and for all, we surrendered to guilt and stepped back in deference to her family. But the memory of this wholly unexpected third appearance of Karla's comet will light up my sky forever.

KEEPING SCORE

When I was a young man teaching college in New England I had a brilliant senior creative-writing student who developed a crush on me and to whose adorably awkward advances I finally surrendered late one Friday afternoon. We had dinner together in a little restaurant outside of town that was frequented mostly by locals; faculty and students tended to stay closer to the campus. We spent the evening in my apartment, made love on the sofa, and fell asleep in my bed. Waking next to this perfect young creature from a wealthy, prominent family filled me with embarrassment, fear, happiness, and pride. Any one of her classmates, including not a few of the girls, would have traded places with me in a minute.

We nurtured a discreet affair that outlasted the semester and might have continued beyond commencement, had she not been snapped up by a Los Angeles technology firm even before receiving her diploma. Thereafter we were reduced to letters, a few self-conscious phone calls, and unrealistic hopes to reunite before eventually she met a rich new guy and disappeared from my life.

During our guilty assignations in my bachelor pad, she proved to be a sweet lover whose inexperience was just one of many charms. We covered all the usual bases and explored a few side trips. That she was easily and joyously orgasmic left plenty of time for pressure-free intercourse or for her to minister to me. The latter turned out to be her favorite pastime; she loved using her gentle hands, *witnessing* (her word) the result, and playing the perfect little nursemaid afterward.

One evening when she was kneeling between my legs making patient sculpting motions, she issued a surprising challenge. "I want you to name all the girls who have ever touched you this way, in chronological order."

I looked up at her and smiled. "Are you sure about that?"

Her response was both nonverbal and entirely persuasive.

"OK," I replied. "Just girls who have made me come this way, or all the girls who have ever touched me?"

"Wow," she smiled, adjusting her grip. "Just girls who have made you come this way."

"Oh, OK." I lay there for a moment trying to ignore what she was doing long enough to organize my thoughts. "Well. Let's see. You do want names?"

"Of course I want names, and real ones. In order. Don't tell me how you met, how long you knew them, or anything else—just their first names."

Although at this point in our relationship I did not expect the girl to move across the continent a few weeks later, neither did I expect our fling to last much longer than that in any case: she was at least ten years younger than I, a math major, and, regardless of her career goals, not likely to remain living in a little college town in the middle of nowhere. I therefore felt I had no reason to invent names of people she would never meet; nor did I feel like taking all night renaming the angels of my past when it was everything I could do to enjoy the present and delay its culmination while going through the list. "OK," I began. "Chloë." I paused, curious as to her reaction. Since there was none, save a widened smile, I continued. "Keira. Elise. Julianne. Cora. Carmen. And Julia, not the same as Julianne. A couple of girls at the beach whose names I don't remember. Jude, and her little sister, Nancy—no, not at the same time. Maureen. Cathy. A different Nancy. Susan. Claire. Katherine, with a *K*. Suzanne. Martha. Therese. Another Cathy. Judy, not Jude. Tammy. Mary. Jennifer. Jane. Justine. Diane. May. Linda. Iva. Joanna. Another Linda. Another Susan. Anna. Brice. Kristen. Maya. Barbara. Grace. Lorraine. And you." I did not mention several call girls and illegitimate masseuses I had patronized during moments of lonely self-indulgence.

My student's timing was perfect. As she reached for the towel, she said, "Later on, when you have a free moment, please write down all those names, total them, and divide by twelve. Next time, I want the names of all the girls who have drunk you."

That list, recited unsteadily the following weekend, came down, as it were, to Keira, Elise, Julianne, Maureen, one of the Cathys, Therese, Judy, Mary, Jennifer, Jane, Anna, Kristen, Maya, Grace, Lorraine, and present company. My assignment was to take the result of the previous arithmetic, add the new list, and divide by nine.

The weekend after that, having assumed her favorite position, the girl whispered, "Now I want the names of all the girls who have let you come inside them."

"With or without a condom?" I asked, grimacing involuntarily.

"What's that look for?"

I reminded my young partner that, unlike her, I had sown my wild oats before the onset of the AIDS epidemic. I had only a few latex-related experiences to report.

"That's even better," she smiled, speeding up gradually.

This list of lists, a still greater threat to my concentration, comprised Keira, Elise, Julianne, both Cathys, Nancy, Katherine, Martha, Therese, Judy, Tammy, Mary, Jennifer, Jane, Justine, Diane, Joanna, one of the Susans, Anna, Brice, Barbara, Grace, Lorraine, and my darling pupil. During our denouement I was instructed to multiply this number by the result of the previous week's problem and divide by six.

The following weekend, which turned out to be our last, she came while riding me on the sofa. Then she asked me to take her to bed and come inside her. Glad to comply, I picked her up without removing myself, carried her to the bedroom, and took my time fulfilling her request. Afterward, I asked her what all the math was about.

"Not a damn thing!" she laughed. "But I'll bet you'll never forget that number!"

The next morning, sitting alone with my tea and the notepad bearing my calculations, I crossed out a decimal point and realized that my thoughtful mathematician had told me her new zip code.

LA BATAILLE
DES BANDES

Marcel Anjou was justifiably proud of the fact that his native France had failed, or, perhaps more accurately, had not bothered to produce a single rock star. At twenty-seven, Marcel had established himself as one of Paris's foremost classical guitarists and as the city's leading interpreter of Django Reinhardt. The Conservatoire de Paris alum was nonetheless always on the lookout for ways to make a decent living: neither sporadic chamber-music concerts nor the odd jazz gig generated enough income to pay Marcel's way.

Marcel had grown up in a home filled with music of all kinds, dominated by his boomer parents' nearly obsessive love for the Beatles. Marcel knew the group's thirteen studio albums and all the singles by heart—guitar parts, harmonies, lyrics, mythology, everything—and it made perfect sense to him that the Beatles were the one rock group that every successive generation around the world appreciated. All the other bands, during and after the British Invasion, were either too sloppy and derivative or too clinical and pretentious to sustain his interest—especially when a file cabinet bursting with serious works from the Renaissance on down to last Thursday was competing for his attention. Marcel saw popular music as the sonic equivalent of fast food and avoided both accordingly.

Family and friends had often told Marcel as a teenager that he bore a striking resemblance to the young John Lennon. Years later, during one of Marcel's financial brainstorming sessions, he considered the overabundance of Beatles tribute bands touring the world and hit on a novel idea: a decidedly French Beatles tribute band that would sing the group's repertoire *en français.* (The "boys" had, after all, thrown their German fans a couple of bones in the forms of "Komm, gib mir deine Hand" and "Sie liebt dich"—recorded, ironically, in Paris. Marcel considered the ugliness of spoken German and wondered how the same society that had developed a language that sounded like an old man spitting up phlegm would go on to give us Bach, Handel, Haydn, Mozart, Beethoven, Schubert, Schumann, and Brahms. *And how do we explain that many people lining up behind a creep like Hitler?* Marcel conjectured that both the Germans and the Japanese were actually extraterrestrial aliens just waiting for their next chance to take over the planet.) Everything else about Marcel's band—clothes, equipment, stage presence—would fit the familiar storyline. Marcel knew that certain songs would require lyrical concessions—he could not imagine singing "Elle vous aime" with a comic refrain of *"Oui, oui, oui!"*— and, in a private Gallic protest against Paul McCartney's touristy pronunciation, Marcel had already decided to forgo the sweet "Michelle." But a few minutes of thought produced the perfect band name: *Les Quatre Fab.* Marcel's girlfriend, a respected graphic artist, produced the iconic bass-drum logo, complete with "drop T." In homage to his musical parents and their liberal politics,

Marcel adopted the stage name *Jean Lenin*. Despite his preference for deep hollow-body jazz guitars, Marcel searched high and low until he found the required little black Rickenbacker 325, a browned Gibson J-160E acoustic-electric, and a blond Epiphone Casino.

Months of phone calls, e-mails, Facebook postings, print ads, and auditions finally brought three other like-minded and physically passable players to Marcel's tiny apartment in the Montmartre neighborhood. (As a Montmartre lad Marcel had been privileged to serve as an extra in the film *Amelie* and would suffer a nagging crush on actress Audrey Tautou.) Bassist Louis Saint-Pierre turned out to be ambidextrous and jumped at the chance to own a laughably overpriced left-handed 1963 Höfner Beatle Bass advertised on eBay. Louis assumed the stage name McCartney himself had used briefly during the Beatles' early days, *Paul Ramon*. Algerian lead guitarist Yousef Ibrahim, who would christen himself *Georges Harrisette,* was appropriately gear-headed and could be found polishing a collection that included all the classic George guitars: a walnut Gretsch Country Gentleman, a red sunburst Ric twelve-string, a psychedelic Fender Stratocaster, and so on. Marcel downplayed the fact that he was a far better guitarist than Yousef and took pains to emulate Lennon's unschooled technique. Typically, nasute drummer Henri La Tour followed in the footsteps of a short-lived earlier candidate and not only played the humble part perfectly but also owned all three models of Ludwig Beatle drum sets: the early Downbeat kit, the larger middle-period Super Classic, both in *de rigueur* Oyster Black Pearl, and the natural-maple Hollywood outfit from the *Abbey Road* days. Henri's sad mother's-son eyes twinkled when he announced his *nom de baguette* as *Ringeau d'Étoile*. Marcel insisted that on the gig his bandmates would refer to one another strictly as Jean, Paul, Georges, and Ringeau. A truckload of Vox amplifiers, a token Vox Continental organ, and many meticulous rehearsals later, Les Quatre Fab embarked on their own magical mystery tour.

The holy grail for a Beatles tribute band is an invitation to perform at one of the international Beatles conventions that take place every year. These nostalgic events draw thousands of paunchy memorabilia-seeking fans, *la crème de la crème* of the tribute-band scene, and lectures or book signings by such Merseyside and Hamburg contemporaries as press agent Tony Barrow, Gerry Marsden (of the Pacemakers), bassist-artist Klaus Voormann, even the unfortunate Pete Best. While one band would be on stage tossing their coiffures, the other musicians would stand around criticizing anything about the performance that fell short of complete authenticity, whether it be an incorrect volume knob, a frayed *Sergeant Pepper* epaulet, or a particularly lame Liverpool accent. Marcel's band would enjoy a distinct advantage in this last department, since *les garçons* refused to speak any sort of English on stage. Two years of nonstop gigging throughout Europe had spread Les Quatre Fab's unique reputation and eventually secured the group a slot at the 2012 Beatlemania Convention at the Hard Rock Hotel and Casino in Las Vegas. Marcel and company were pleased to learn that the presenter would provide the proper drums, amps, and P.A., as well as each player's monitor (the

Beatles themselves would have appreciated this final product of a later era, so they could have heard themselves over the jet-engine screams of teenage girls); Les Quatre would need bring only their rare guitars and their ordinary drumsticks.

On the appointed evening, Les Quatre Fab took the stage, plugged in, and smiled at their adoring tote-bag-toting followers. Louis Saint-Pierre had scarcely finished shouting the *"Un, deux, trois, QUATRE!"* that introduced "Je l'ai vu debout là" when his lips brushed the microphone, sparks flew around his head and from his amplifier jack, and the young musician fell to the floor, severing the neck of his fragile Höfner. Louis's friends rushed to his aid, but his scorched skin had turned blue and he was not breathing. Paramedics arrived in a few minutes and pronounced that, in accordance with Beatle legend, Paul was dead.

The absence in the building of another French-speaking ambidextrous bassist notwithstanding, the three surviving bandmates were too dispirited to consider going on with the show. Their union contract guaranteed payment in full, since they had done their part in good faith and Louis's electrocution certainly was not their fault. Marcel's Paris lawyer assured him by cell phone that she would determine exactly whose fault it was. The guys returned to their hotel rooms, packed their bags, and in the morning returned to L.A. to begin the long journey back to France.

Les Quatre Fab disbanded temporarily, both out of respect for Louis Saint-Pierre and in observance of the daunting prospect of replacing him in the City of Light.

They agreed to try again after a suitable mourning period, though none of the guys had a feel for how long that might be. Marcel resumed his spartan schedule of classical and jazz gigs and, to help pay off the credit cards with which he had amassed his expensive gear, freelanced as a waiter and museum guide. Marcel's mood brightened only once, on the evening when he was channeling Django in a little club and actor Johnny Depp walked in carrying a guitar case. The two jammed into the wee hours, but the star's handlers whisked him away before Marcel could offer his business card.

Nearly every singing guitarist who has performed with amplification has experienced an occasional moment when an ungrounded circuit here or there will produce a mild electric shock: the typical scenario has the player experimentally touching his strings and the mike simultaneously, feeling a slight sizzle to the fingers, pausing to correct the ground situation (which usually means flipping a ground switch, reversing a plug, or choosing a different outlet), and continuing on with the gig. But a shock capable of causing death is rare; usually it is the result of performing outdoors in a storm, an obviously stupid situation that no musician should accept. Louis Saint-Pierre's untimely demise in a new, first-class venue, at the hands of standard equipment that other players had used uneventfully throughout the day, produced a series of lawsuits and investigations that would outlive many a rock band.

Meanwhile, Marcel pursued his other work and reminded himself not to let Les Quatre Fab languish indefinitely: even in a business based on distant memories, the public attention span was brief.

Yousef Ibrahim's dark Mediterranean features had not been entirely out of place in Les Quatre Fab. George Harrison's seminal explorations into Eastern culture and religion had opened the "quiet Beatle" to more than his share of gentle satire. The George character in Eric Idle's beloved *Rutles* parody was played by Ricky Fataar, a South African musician of Indonesian descent; and Justin Long, the uncredited actor who played George in the hilarious *Walk Hard: The Dewey Cox Story,* is similarly swarthy (Long's grandmother was Sicilian). Inevitably, not everyone has found this "ethnic stereotyping" to be funny.

Yousef and drummer Henri La Tour's predecessor actually had been Marcel's first hires for the band. Each of them knew that finding a lefty bass player with a high voice and cherubic good looks would be a tall order, and none was surprised that Louis Saint-Pierre's arrival followed many disappointing auditions. The only other candidate who had come close to cutting the gig was dismissed primarily for musical reasons; but the clincher was that "Polythene" Pham Sinh, the chatty only child of the Vietnamese ambassador to France, looked no more like Paul McCartney than anyone else from his quarter of the planet. Les Quatre Fab were already pushing their luck with their French-language gimmick, and the unspoken consensus at Pham's audition was that welcoming *two* band members of obviously non-English ancestry would be asking too much of the audience. The guys listened patiently as Pham paraded the knowledge of music and electronics that typifies a rich kid who can afford to throw equipment at his problems. That Pham not only lost the audition after grueling weeks teaching himself to play left-handed but also turned out to be ten minutes late in bidding on the '63 Höfner that Louis Saint-Pierre had found on eBay offended the little pest. But what really broke Pham's heart was that he had lost the chance to declare his sexual attraction to Marcel Anjou, whose classical career Pham had followed for years.

Pham Sinh began stalking Les Quatre Fab, showing up at all their European gigs, no matter how distant from Paris, standing near the stage, trying to make eye contact with the players, accosting them during breaks to talk shop and pretend he was just another busy musician with a night off (Pham could have expected to live happily unemployed throughout his pampered existence), and taking every opportunity to spend a few minutes alone with Marcel. The responsibilities of bandleading gave Marcel plenty of reasons to escape Pham's presence, but the guy was becoming a serious nuisance. For public-relations reasons, Marcel's lawyer advised against seeking a restraining order unless Pham became violent, which seemed the least likely thing in the world. When Pham was, for the first time in two years, absent from the edge of the stage in faraway Las Vegas, Marcel and his mates merely smiled at one another in relief.

What Les Quatre Fab did not know was that "Polythene" Pham led a double life as a female impersonator in Paris nightclubs and had arrived in Vegas dressed persuasively like one of the slinky hookers who cruised the Strip hotels. Pham had gone through the kitchen to make his/her way backstage, made friends with the sound crew, and awaited a moment during the rushed activity between acts to sneak onto the darkened stage and sabotage Louis Saint-Pierre's rented Vox Super Beatle amplifier.

Pham Sinh still did not get the gig, of course, but he did get picked up for solicitation after the panicked monitor engineer told the irksome freak for the third time to bug off. Les Quatre were back in their Paris beds by the time Vegas cops analyzed a singed screwdriver and a pair of pliers bearing minute copper-wire fragments like those they had found in Pham Sinh's purse.

In February 2014, after Marcel finally had tracked down a suitable new bass player, Les Quatre Fab were invited to play the *Late Show with David Letterman* in New York to help celebrate the fiftieth anniversary of the Beatles' debut performance in the Ed Sullivan Theater. A few minutes before dress rehearsal, Letterman sidled over to Marcel and told him the group would be joined by a special guest. The guys looked at one another and shrugged.

In the next moment, Paul McCartney strode on stage and strapped on the most famous bass guitar in history. He smiled at his stunned accompanists and said, "I assume you blokes know me song 'Michelle.' F minor, *oui*?" The Beatle was not accustomed to hearing the word *non* and did not await a response. He stepped to the microphone and counted off the tune in a much-improved French accent.

LIBRARY
DAYDREAM

CAST OF CHARACTERS:
- *UNNAMED YOUNG FEMALE CIRCULATION STAFFER*
- *UNNAMED MIDDLE-AGED MALE NOVELIST MOONLIGHTING AS A CATALOGER*
- *FRANCINE, A SEMILITERATE MIDDLE-AGED FEMALE SUPERVISOR*
- *MYRNA, A SEMILITERATE MIDDLE-AGED CHILDREN'S LIBRARIAN (OFFSTAGE)*
- *UNNAMED ELDERLY FEMALE LIBRARY DIRECTOR*

TIME: THE PRESENT

PLACE: A SMALL-TOWN COUNTY PUBLIC LIBRARY

STAFFER: I found this wedged between two Spanish dictionaries in the reference section. Its spine label is missing, and the barcode is torn in half. Where do you want it?

CATALOGER: Well, I realize your generation has a slightly different take on reality than mine, but I think even you would agree that a children's book about a talking dinosaur is *probably* fiction.

STAFFER: Right, but—

CATALOGER: Now, of course, if it were about a talking dinosaur and a vampire having a ménage à trois with a handsome prince disguised as a time-traveling werewolf who writes worthless comic books—oh, I mean *graphic novels*—that, obviously, would go in with the young-adult knitting manuals.

STAFFER WALKS AWAY, PERPLEXED.

SUPERVISOR: This is all a big joke to you, isn't it?

CATALOGER: Yes, actually. And the only thing standing between you and the breadline is my need for health insurance.

SUPERVISOR: Excuse me?

CATALOGER: The worst sort of amateur is the one who can't stop saying, "We're all professionals here." If I were to tell my friends in the media what I know about this pathetic culture of mediocrity, incompetence, fraud, cronyism, stupidity, waste, and failure that you rednecks have been guarding with your lives for the past hundred years, you and half a dozen other local peasants would find your fat asses on the front page of the newspaper in a scandal that would make that idiot in the county administrator's office who sold all those stolen cell phones look like Mary Poppins.

SUPERVISOR GASPS IN HORROR.

CATALOGER: Respect is earned. I earned yours walking in the door. What could you possibly do at this point to earn mine?

SUPERVISOR: Well, I could write you up for insubordination.

CATALOGER: So now we're in the Marine Corps? No, that merely would confirm what I learned my first day: that you have no more business working here than you do piloting a spacecraft. In the real world, people who wouldn't know Hemingway from Shakespeare work at K-Mart or McDonald's, not a publicly funded library. Your presence here is a slap in the face to every taxpayer in the county. Just because we use the same application form they do at Public Works doesn't mean that I should be operating a backhoe or that you should be taking up space here, with the blessing of our so-called superiors. Writing me up also would *guarantee* the scandal of which I spoke before. Not to mention that without me you'd actually have to start doing your job, and everyone knows you don't want that. In the unlikely event that we ever get some legitimate leadership, you'd better have your bags packed.

SUPERVISOR WALKS AWAY, FRUSTRATED BY A BYZANTINE BUBBA SYSTEM DESIGNED AND

PERPETUATED BY UNSOPHISTICATED PERSONS SUCH AS HERSELF.

LATER IN THE DAY, SUPERVISOR UNPACKS SEVERAL BOXES OF EXPENSIVE NEW BOOKS ORDERED BY SEMILITERATE CHILDREN'S LIBRARIAN, ON WHOM SUPERVISOR CUSTOMARILY SHOWERS FAVORITISM AT THE EXPENSE OF FOUR AND A HALF OTHER LIBRARY BRANCHES; SHE BEGINS PLACING THE BOOKS ON CATALOGER'S DESK FOR PROCESSING.

CATALOGER, AFTER PROCESSING THE FIRST BOX: Do you have anything over there worth collecting, or are we all about Myrna?

SUPERVISOR PRETENDS NOT TO HAVE HEARD CATALOGER'S WISECRACK.

LIBRARY DIRECTOR, THE NEXT DAY: I don't appreciate the way Francine says you spoke to her.

CATALOGER: And?

LIBRARY DIRECTOR: And I demand that you apologize to her at once.

CATALOGER: I'll apologize to that cow when you step up and start showing some goddamned integrity. You might begin by terminating all these uneducated hillbillies you have waddling around here occupying unnecessary positions that anywhere else would require a master's degree. There are published scholars in this town selling timeshares and bartending so that people like Francine can impersonate librarians at public expense. She spends fully half of every day sitting around jabbering with her dumbass girlfriends about their self-induced health problems, food, their dying relatives, *American Idol,* food, their loser kids, cheesy action movies, their insane marriages, and did I mention food? They come in late and leave early every single day. They abuse the sick-leave and vacation policies at every opportunity. They begin each morning with breakfast on the patrons' nickel, followed immediately by a discussion of what they'll order for lunch; then they pretend to work till the highlight of their day, lunch, an hour after which they start dipping into the huge bags of snacks on their desks. They eat more in eight hours than a healthy person consumes in a week. They—

LIBRARY DIRECTOR: All right, that's it, I'm writing you up.

CATALOGER: Don't bother. I'm going to make your day: I quit, effective immediately. Don't say another fucking word to me. In ten minutes my key to the building will be placed atop that aftermath-of-an-Afghan-air-raid that Francine calls a desk. Oh, and unless you feel like waking to a news crew on your front lawn tomorrow and every day thereafter for the foreseeable future, you might want to consider moving to China.

CATALOGER WAKES FROM HIS DAYDREAM AND RETURNS HIS ATTENTION TO THE STACK OF

"GRAPHIC NOVELS" ON HIS DESK, AS SUPERVISOR FALLS ASLEEP AT HERS.

CURTAIN

MADEIRA IN TRANSLATION

I met Madeira on a Caribbean island in 1984. She was visiting the couple with whom I was vacationing. She was Brazilian. Unlike Nathalia, her bilingual cousin, Madeira spoke only a few words of English. We nevertheless learned our own method of communication.

She was smashing. Short-cropped, gleaming chocolate hair; a golden, cheerful face; lovely dark eyes; a graceful neck. Perfect body: tastily muscular shoulders, firm little breasts, trim waist, cute round ass, sleek legs—even her feet were sexy and adorable. She was a twenty-three-year-old grad student and part-time fashion model.

We felt each other immediately. Since our foursome went on a long day trip together, Madeira and I composed an intriguing blind date, each of us tripping over our modest bits of the other's language. We rode in the backseat, occasionally writing to each other in my notebook. By the evening it was clear we wanted to meet again, alone. We arranged it for the next day. Madeira's teasing cousin kindly loaned us her car.

Our first stop was a local bookstore, to pick up a Portuguese-English dictionary. I would leave this with Madeira to commemorate our achingly brief union.

We drove to the beach, strolled about, and conversed to the extent we could before sitting down in the sand for the long, silent moment of truth. We watched the sea for several seconds, checking each other out as discreetly as possible. Finally we turned and kissed.

We wanted each other badly, but it was broad daylight and we did not know our surroundings. We spent the rest of the afternoon taking pictures, exploring the island, and yearning.

As dusk fell we dropped by the house. Nathalia sized us up and, again, put her intuition to good use. She told us of a nearby wildlife refuge that was unattended after dark.

Madeira and I pulled onto the dirt road that wound through a canopied wonderland. As night descended, our car was invisible. In anticipation, we embraced.

Undressed in short order, we touched, our excitement racing. In the tropical heat, all the glass fogged over and the car became a slippery steam bath. Had we opened a window, mosquitoes would have devoured us.

Madeira told me she was not on the pill; she said further that she did not have much experience. I took this to mean that we should save intercourse for the next day, since I had managed to buy the dictionary but not the accessories. We explored each other long into the night, trembling in preorgasmic anticipation. Madeira's English seemed well on its way as I knelt kissing her swollen flower:

"I cannot wait! I cannot wait!"

The following morning we drove back to the beach and booked a room in a high-rise hotel. We had a spectacular view of the sea. Of course we saw precious little of it.

In seconds we were naked, savoring the feel of clean sheets and our fragrant skin. She was simply spectacular to look at, the kind of girl I normally would only have dreamed of touching. And in her I relished something I had noticed previously in the sweaty car:

Madeira was exceptionally sweet. I stayed on her forever, darting to every reachable spot. She lay trembling in ecstasy, holding herself open to offer all her sensitivity. She came over and over again.

Our intercourse was a little disappointing, simply because the only condoms I had found were apparently designed for some unrelated industrial use. I was making love with one of the most beautiful women I had ever seen, hardly able to feel her. Just holding Madeira was more than I could have hoped for on this holiday, though, so I devoted myself to pleasing her.

Madeira had never been entered from behind. As I eased her into position, I asked, "Are you OK?"

"I do not know. You are teacher."

Later Madeira climbed on top. By then she was on fire, bearing down and fucking me with breathtaking passion. In a few minutes her face lit up. She actually began laughing. I thought she suddenly had seen the absurdity of our impulsive relationship.

"I am coming! Ooh, I am *here!* Do you feel it?"

I still do.

After the lovely girl descended to me and her pulsations resolved, she slid over to my side. We held each other a long time before she reached down and pulled the empty condom from my throbbing erection.

Madeira knelt between my legs and took me in her mouth. She was such a vision of beauty that I could not look away. Her own eyes were closed most of the time, but she showed no sign of embarrassment as she lavished herself on me. Freed of latex, I celebrated. She was holding me in her left hand but performing all her magic orally. Her wet hair dancing against sculptured cheekbones, graceful fingers wrapped around me, her gorgeous body drawn up into my center transfixed me. She took my crown deep, withdrawing it and running her lips quickly around it as if saving a melting ice-cream cone; she paused and used broad strokes of her pretty pink tongue up and down, darting and tapping with tender urgency. After several amazing minutes my orgasm swept up like a crashing wave.

"I will come now," I enunciated.

Madeira pulled back and became utterly still. Our eyes met, and for a moment she did not seem to know what to do. Finally she began moving her hand as we locked each other in our gaze. In that instant I would have married her straight away. She stroked me lovingly until long after it was over. Finally she looked down, smiled, and kissed my pulsating shaft.

"Wait," she whispered, as she rose and walked to the bathroom. Observing those few motions was in itself worth the price of admission. Madeira returned with a warm, wet washcloth and a towel. She lay down beside me, supporting herself on her left elbow.

"Feel better now?" she smiled mischievously, surveying the prodigious result of our two-day foreplay.

"You are so beautiful. I almost came in your mouth."

"I have not tasted," Madeira replied. She dipped her fingertip in one of the streams and touched her tongue. She smiled. "Next time."

"Perhaps, yes."

Alas, next time never came. Madeira and I said goodbye a day later and returned to our lives. We had exchanged addresses and phone numbers, and we even had talked of vacationing together again. But each of us knew it was unlikely.

About a week later my phone rang.

"I am Madeira," chirped the bright voice on the line. I was thrilled. We spoke our halting patois for a while, agonizing in the limitations of words, the only substance passing between us being that we longed to be in each other's arms. A few calls and letters followed, and Madeira disappeared into the world.

Some years later Nathalia told me Madeira had married a guy in São Paulo. I remembered the gentle girl's comment that stereotypically macho Latin men offended her. I hope she found an exception. I hope he knows what a prize he won.

THE MANSFIELD EFFECT

Brenda and I were both theater majors, and we used to flirt in the corridors. One night she accompanied me to my off-campus apartment.

Brenda was a brassy blonde who oozed sex. She was my first encounter with enormous tits.

Brenda was not at all overweight, just tall and incredibly stacked. She had the kind of centerfold body that drove my father's generation mad. I had always preferred dark, petite women with dancer's proportions. Brenda and I knew that the only lasting value of our rendezvous would be a knowing smile in the hallway.

Brenda played the waiting game with purposeful delight. She would not let me under her clothes for a good hour. Her heavy-duty brassiere heaved against my grasp like a pair of lurching submarines trapped beneath an ice floe. Only after we were in bed, both fully aroused, would Brenda peel off one item at a time. When finally we were naked, I wanted her so badly that I almost did not see the humor of her two great orbs galumphing all over the place.

"Mmmm," she moaned, "and I thought you were just a stupid *actor*."

We satisfied each other enough, but overall I came away unimpressed. As a lover Brenda was a bit of a bore. If my experience with others like her is any indication, there is more than a handful of truth in the adage that endowment has little to do with enjoyment.

MINTON AND
MISTRAL

Born to loving Irish-American parents in Boston on February 2, 1992, Minton and Mistral Quarles were conjoined twins. As such they were the subject of fascination and study as infants, and the medical establishment would follow their progress through life.

At first appearance the twins looked like a two-headed hermaphrodite. As their parents had done, Minton and Mistral came into the world with a wisp of light red hair and characteristic cream-white skin. Each had fine facial features; Minton would grow to be as handsome as his sister was beautiful. From the neck down their body appeared almost normal, with two arms and two legs, but with extremely wide shoulders to accommodate their two heads. The twins nearly could face each other directly. Excepting their sex organs, Minton and Mistral shared the overworked internal systems of a single person and were not expected to live long lives.

Lindsey and Marianne Quarles were wealthy enough to educate Minton and Mistral at home and in a small private school for kids with special needs. Throughout childhood the twins seemed amazingly happy. Intelligent and perceptive, Minton and Mistral developed not only the telepathic behaviors of twins but also a wry sense of humor; their first common joke parodied their counterintuitive surname. Minton was naturally left-handed and his sister the opposite, which meant they could address joint games and projects with unusual dexterity. They learned to accommodate each other's complex mental, emotional, and physical reality. Their social life was a lesson in tolerance, since one sibling's friends necessarily had to get along with the other.

Minton and Mistral's independent sexualities provided epic speculation for doctors, family, and friends. Minton's small but fully functional penis was located just above Mistral's clitoris. The girl's vagina was otherwise normal. Her labia had appropriated Minton's scrotum, so the boy's testicles would never descend. Mistral's unremarkable cervix, ovaries, and uterus left adequate room for Minton's little prostate and Cowper's glands and seminal vesicles.

No one anticipated the milestone of puberty with more eagerness and uncertainty than the twins themselves. They giggled when a small crop of strawberry-blond hair appeared between their legs, and they agreed not to let it grow out of control. Minton was less excited than Mistral at the formation of two soft little breasts, and the girl expressed similarly mixed feelings about her brother's enlarged penis and its ever more frequent erections. After experiencing these awkward changes for a few months, the two realized they must not only accept but also celebrate their unique situation.

The twins' best friend was an artistically inclined girl their age named Dido Franck, whose precocious interest in sex had begun at home: she surreptitiously had observed her older brother masturbating and soon thereafter began doing so herself. Dido was naturally on high alert in Minton and Mistral's presence. She described her "research" to the twins and made no secret of her curiosity. One afternoon after school she talked them into a brief mutual showing: they stood naked opposite each other in the twins' private bathroom and stared until the word *normal* had lost all meaning. After Dido went home for supper, Minton and Mistral realized their queasy moment of truth had arrived.

The twins learned immediately that it was impossible for one of them to masturbate without arousing the other. Typically, the boy showed more interest in this activity than the girl, but Mistral never objected to Minton's new habit or its untidy aftermath. Usually she would join in before her brother's orgasm, and the two even learned to come at the same time. Occasionally one sibling would wake the other in the middle of the night hungry for release. Eventually they acknowledged that nothing between them could be taboo and gave up trying to keep their hands to themselves. Minton and Mistral quickly overcame their guilt and confusion because they had no choice. Invariably their private sessions ended in joyous laughter.

Later in their teens, Minton and Mistral discussed the challenges of dating and agreed that seeing two other people would be too complicated. Each twin felt heterosexual, but their situation demanded extraordinary candor. Mistral's desire to be with another boy did not sit well with Minton, self-conscious as he was about his unspectacular cock and his invisible balls; but he promised his sister he would never deny her fulfillment should the opportunity present itself. Similarly, Mistral agreed to share any girl willing to explore with her unique sibling. In an ever-changing world, the possibilities for encounters with empathetic transgender partners were encouraging. The twins had both welcomed and lamented the physical impossibility of having intercourse with each other.

The obvious first choice for a sex partner for Minton and Mistral was their friend Dido, who reacted to their invitation by exclaiming, "God, I thought you'd never ask!"

Their meetings after school and on weekends were marked by intense discoveries and a rarified intimacy that Dido would translate into poems, a short story, a novel, and finally a screenplay.

One of Dido's favorite pastimes was imagining which delicious young Hollywood couple would leap at the chance to embody her computer-generated fantasy world. The project so captivated her that she moved west and enrolled at the UCLA School of Theatre, Film, and Television.

The acclaimed independent film Dido's debut screenplay would germinate after the writer had pounded the Los Angeles pavement for two years turned out to be not just a love story but also a memorial. After a promising first reading with an A-list cast, Dido returned briefly to Boston hoping to break the good news to her friends. Unable to reach them by telephone, she arrived at their apartment door to find it sealed with yellow tape.

Having failed to contact the twins' parents, Dido phoned the police. Since she was not immediate family, Dido received only evasion and hung up after being transferred to voice mail.

The twins had bragged to Dido about Ali Ravindra, the wunderkind specialist at Harvard Medical School who had shepherded their early development. After many minutes on hold, Dido was devastated to learn that Minton and Mistral Quarles had been found dead the previous evening, hanged from an exposed beam below the ceiling of their apartment.

Late that night, in an alley near Boston Symphony Hall, the cops arrested forty-two-year-old Evan Greer, a yoga instructor from Sedona, Arizona. DNA and hemp fibers found in Greer's backpack matched those from the rope used to kill Minton and Mistral Quarles.

With the *Globe* on her lap the next morning, Dido grabbed her cell phone and roused the director of her film from a deep sleep, asking her to suspend production for a few days so Dido could rewrite her ending. Dido's research into her friends' deaths would obviate the need for any sort of fiction.

Two years after Dido had moved to L.A. to solicit investors and to lay the groundwork for *Minton & Mistral,* her adventurous but still loveless friends answered an online advertisement for a tantric sensual trainer. Thirty-two-year-old Isis Greer and her Svengali husband Evan traveled the country giving workshops and private sessions to individuals and couples seeking fuller and more spiritual sex lives. The two therapists typically spent the spring and fall in Sedona, winter in Florida, and summer in New England. They had been in greater Boston for two weeks when Mistral telephoned and booked a session with Isis. Startled but intrigued to hear of her new client's physical condition, Isis tried to persuade Mistral to try a session with both her and Evan; but Minton insisted that his sister invite only Isis to this initial appointment.

Minton and Mistral's two-hour simultaneous full-body orgasm in their apartment on that brilliant June morning with Isis was so amazing that they set up a weekly schedule. By July, both siblings were in love with Isis, and, despite her rigorous professional standards, she had developed serious feelings for them. Since Isis always compared notes with Evan on their clients, he knew everything about the libidinous twins except what it felt like to be with them. Isis's month of coaxing had not disabused Minton of his admitted homophobia. Mistral, anxious over Isis's planned return to Sedona that September, had added her voice to their trainer's. Finally Minton agreed to include Evan in their penultimate session, during the last week of August. If it went well, the twins would decide whether they wanted Isis all to themselves one more time.

Evan himself telephoned and set the date. It was the first time either of the twins had heard his voice.

On the appointed afternoon, Evan showed up at Minton and Mistral's address alone. He explained that Isis was running late and would join them soon. He went to the kitchen as if he owned the place and began brewing a pot of herbal tea. Minton and Mistral sat on the sofa feeling increasingly uncomfortable as the minutes ticked by and the strange man who seemed nothing like his gentle, intuitive partner paced hurriedly about their home as if seeking a lost set of car keys.

While waiting for the water to boil, Evan approached Minton and Mistral and asked, "Well, shall we get comfortable?"

As the two sat silently struggling to give Isis's husband the benefit of the doubt, Evan abruptly removed his pullover to reveal a tight, athletic torso.

Minton and Mistral did not budge.

Evan laughed softly and stepped back. "I seem to have caught you two a bit off guard, haven't I?" he smiled. "I'm sorry. Isis has told me so much about you that—"

The teakettle began whistling, and Evan sprinted to the kitchen.

The twins looked at each other and shrugged.

"I guess he has a different style," Mistral whispered, smiling meekly.

Minton did not respond, except to glare toward the sound of a stirring spoon.

When Evan returned carrying two steaming, fragrant cups, Mistral noticed the detailed bulge in the trainer's thin white cotton sweatpants. She accepted her cup in trembling fingers and saw that her brother's hand was no steadier.

Evan sat in a chair opposite them and summarized what Isis had told him about their sessions, punctuating his talk with breezy humor and tantric insights. Several times Minton and Mistral glanced between the wall clock and the door, expecting Isis's recognizable three taps. Evan was still droning on when the twins spilled the remains of their tea and simultaneously collapsed in a deep sleep.

Evan assessed the twins' convenient position on the sofa and smiled at them for a while. Then he kicked off his sandals, stood, and removed his pants.

Minutes later, Minton and Mistral's strangely beautiful semiconscious naked body was covered in their blood and in both men's semen. Evan tested the thick overhead beam, strung up his rope, and put his Bikram training to good use as he hoisted the medical phenomena to the ceiling. He stood waiting until their breathing had stopped. Evan walked to the bathroom, showered, returned to the living room, put his clothes back on, and left the apartment.

In a dark corner of the alley near Symphony Hall, Evan Greer undressed, took out a separately bagged change of clothes and shoes, and stuffed his sandals, sweatpants, and pullover into the backpack. He took out a cigarette lighter. Evan was just about to torch the backpack and toss it into a large trash receptacle when the police surprised him with guns drawn.

Realizing the damning nature of the evidence he had left behind, Evan made a full confession at the police station. "Oh, yes, I killed it," he told his interrogators. "That thing was evil, a practical joke against nature, and I put it out of its misery."

Evan Greer had no history of violence, bigotry, or antisocial behavior. The police psychiatrist concluded that the holistic mentor simply had acted on suppressed jealous rage.

When Isis Greer learned what her husband had done, she returned to Sedona, donated Evan's belongings to charity, divorced him, and never again spoke of him. The only other time Isis even saw his name was when she read that Evan had been sentenced to two consecutive lifetimes in a prison for the criminally insane.

Conjoined twins occur about once in every two hundred thousand births, and they rarely survive childhood. Minton and Mistral Quarles were twenty-two when they were murdered, two blocks from the genetic research center that bears their parents' names. Doctors estimated that the twins could have lived another two to four years, before their shared heart gave out.

NORA IN THE OFFICE

We were section mates in various college ensembles. Nora was an unspectacular blonde. But she was sweet and, when we were alone, suggestive. Our playful laughter had hardly subsided one evening when nature found us on the backseat. We spent a hotel weekend together on tour, and the following year we met a couple of times in my apartment.

Our sex was not memorable, but it had another dimension. We were more than friends. We worked together every day. We respected each other's professional abilities. In bed we visualized each other on stage. With Nora I discovered the unique thrill of fucking a colleague.

OLD VIENNA

A nonfiction interlude

I know what you're thinking: here comes another ode to the city of Mozart and the Waltz King. I missed that tour, unfortunately, though my parents and older sister, Carol, lived there for two years shortly before I was born in 1951. Dad, a high-school principal and teacher of science and history in his native Pittsburgh, had been sent to Austria by the federal government to supervise an innovative student-exchange program. From there he went to Washington to continue in this capacity at the State Department. Apparently my parents' happy Viennese tenure inspired them to choose as their D.C.-area home the neighboring town of Vienna, Virginia. This, then, is a random collection of memories of a once charming village that today survives as a baby boomers' Facebook page.

Vienna was little more than a dirt crossroads when Mom and Dad bought an aging two-story house on Old Courthouse Road. Nearby Tysons Corner, that is, the intersection of State Routes 7, called Leesburg Pike, and 123, known as Chain Bridge Road or Dolley Madison Highway in McLean to the east, Maple Avenue in Vienna itself, and Ox Road to the west, was marked by a little red butcher's shop that served what then was the middle of nowhere. Today Tysons is part of a sprawling commercial eyesore that continues consuming farmland out past Dulles Airport and nearly all the way to the old Civil War town of Leesburg itself. (The indoor shopping mall called Tysons Corner Center, built in 1967, was among the first of its kind in the United States.) Throughout the sixties and seventies Dad had lamented selling the Old Courthouse Road house, since keeping it would have made us millionaires. As recently as 1999, the spot where the house stood was a Merrill Lynch office, the good news being that someone had been kind enough to retain the old oak trees that had shaded our front yard.

Our house on Old Courthouse Road was a lovely unpainted stucco building with gables, heavy forest-green doors, indoor archways, art-deco fixtures, a flagstone patio, and other features reminiscent of the Truman administration. (Grandfatherly Eisenhower was the first president of whom I had any personal awareness. One sunny afternoon Dad said hello to Vice President Nixon and his family as they toured the quiet area in their convertible. Years later Dad would remember Nixon as a good president who simply got caught. That's when I gave up arguing with Republicans.) The house was surrounded by woods—Dad liked to repeat the story of the time he was burying an old pet dog and was spared a copperhead bite when the snake went for Dad's shovel instead of his leg— and our nearest neighbor was about a block away. I saw my first example of poverty just across the street: a large, dirty family squatted in the basement that was all that remained of an unfinished house. My little brother, Charles, and I played with their kids and learned quickly not to repeat their vulgar vocabulary.

When I was about six I witnessed an actual fistfight one afternoon, between, oddly enough, two women: the matriarch of the squatter family and another woman I didn't know were going at each other in the middle of the street. It was the strangest thing I'd ever seen and seemed to happen in slow motion. I remember noticing that the weak sounds of their wild, ungainly blows didn't match the choreographed Foley punches I'd heard on early television shows such as *Broken Arrow* and *The Lone Ranger*. The fight lasted a few minutes, until the two participants just stopped and walked away from each other.

Around the corner was a small general store that delivered our groceries. The owner and my mom became friends. Since we had plenty of space for people and other creatures, Mom impulsively agreed to adopt one of the grocer's white baby goats. Mom eschewed the obvious name *Billy* in favor of the far more imaginative name *Willie*. Willie was great fun for a few weeks, until he contracted some disease and refused to eat. Sitting on the floor in my bedroom one night with tears in my eyes, I watched Willie die in Mom's arms as she held a milk bottle to his quivering pink mouth.

Next door to the "hole" across the street lived my first friend, D., a blonde girl my age. Next door to her lived a toothless old woman named Effie who sold Mom eggs and cucumbers, the latter pronounced *kyoomers*. I don't remember a single other resident in that neighborhood. A mile or so down the road in the opposite direction from the general store was another, slightly larger general store. The day my family inadvertently drove off and left me there for several minutes provided many a chuckle around the old Thanksgiving table.

Also in that direction was Freedom Hill School, where

I began elementary school. Dad chose the school parking lot in which to give my sister her first driving lesson in our powder-blue 1953 Chevrolet four-door sedan. For reasons unknown, they agreed to let me ride along in the backseat. Carol did so well that Dad agreed to let her drive home. Turning back onto Old Courthouse Road, Carol misjudged the curve and went off the road, bumping into a neighbor's mailbox. To me this fender bender seemed positively apocalyptic. I ran the block or so home, meeting Mom at the end of our driveway and sounding the alarm: "We crashed, we crashed!" Completing the cycle years later, I would take my own driver's test in Carol's powder-blue 1967 Mustang convertible and would barely pass because the cop in the passenger seat took stop signs more literally than anyone with whom I'd ever ridden.

Speaking of civil war, there apparently was an actual Battle of Vienna on June 17, 1861, centered on the railroad that would run through the center of town until my teens. We attended a reenactment in the early sixties; I can still smell the gunpowder that local historians fired in the general direction of an old locomotive and passenger car they had parked on the tracks between the Community Center and the Safeway store. Today the track bed, named the Washington and Old Dominion Trail, is a paved bicyclist's paradise that runs forty-five miles from Alexandria to the east all the way out to the piedmont town of Purcellville.

Throughout my childhood we employed a middle-aged black housekeeper named Estelle who was as much a part of the family as any of us. With quiet dignity she deflected the embarrassing racist comments some of my less enlightened acquaintances uttered in her hearing; most offensive was one of my first bandmates' calling me a "nigger lover" as we rehearsed pop songs that owed their existence to Africa. We visited Estelle's home once when she was too sick to get out of bed; I was amazed to discover a whole section of town devoid of white people and of whitewashed houses. Estelle attended a local Pentecostal church and often hummed gospel tunes to accompany endless beige wicker baskets of ironing. When those baskets were empty we'd sit in them in the laundry room and pretend to row them down the Potomac.

In the days before Maple Avenue emerged as Vienna's main commercial artery, the center of town was where Church Street intersected the railroad tracks. Facing the tracks were the stately Vienna Trust Company (then the only bank in town), a feed store, a smelly chemical lab, an automotive repair shop, and a small quarry whose dusty red silo rose high in the air. Two blocks of Church Street comprised a few other establishments: the Full Cry Shop, a women's clothing store that catered to the equestrian community of nearby Oakton; Curly's, the working-class men's outfitter where we bought our jeans, flannels, and winter boots; the post office; and of course the Family Music Centre, where I took my first drum lessons and became a regular and not altogether welcome researcher. At the corner of Church Street and Lawyers Road sat the old wooden Knights of Columbus Hall, where my band would discover the thrill of natural echo. Just across Lawyers Road was the private home from which we would be ejected one night for drowning out the insects with electric guitars. On the hill behind Church Street rose a cozy neighborhood of neat brick houses and majestic old trees.

We had an attic that I never saw and a basement that, with its many dark, mysterious features, was one of my special places. We called this room the cellar and for some reason didn't begin using the word *basement* until we moved across town in 1959. My favorite memories of the cellar are of private moments with Dad, building and operating electric-train layouts and watching him tinker with tools. I can still hear the clickety-clack of my green-and-yellow diesel locomotive rounding the corners, disappearing into snowcapped tunnels, flying past miniature shops and lampposts, accompanied by the unforgettable smells of a warm transformer and damp concrete.

We had no air-conditioning in those days, and I remember many a sweaty night upstairs in my bed, shifting constantly to find a cool spot, soothing myself with the drone of the impotent window fan. The Beatles would already have conquered the world by the time Dad splurged on a single window AC unit, mounted in the dining room of our next house.

Our move in the blazing summer of 1959 to the new planned community of Vienna Woods (another pathetic nod to the real Vienna) was well timed in one respect and not so fortuitous in another: (1) our beloved cellar was prone to flooding, and I suppose my parents got tired of hoisting one valuable thing up on blocks after discarding some other thing for which it was too late; and (2) that also was the year Dad was appointed cultural attaché to Israel. We rented our brand-new house, for which Dad paid thirteen thousand dollars, to a family that showed the place considerably less respect than we had, and would, on our return three years later.

In the early sixties a new shopping center was built on the opposite side of town, across from my junior high school, Henry Thoreau Intermediate, and near the old town of Dunn Loring. The parking lot was shaped like an amphitheater, rising on the hill above the building, and in the months leading to the grand opening it was a great place to indulge my short-lived enthusiasm for skateboarding. For many kids a skateboard still consisted of a two-foot plank and four metal wheels cannibalized from a pair of clip-on roller skates. I considered my new commercial version, polished oak with cushioned red rubber wheels—still a miniature by today's standards—to be the Stradivarius of skateboards. But the finger-conscious musician in me abandoned this dangerous diversion well before the strip mall's ribbon-cutting ceremony.

This decision coincided with a friend's developing interest in photography. Kodak Brownie in hand, he would pose several of us around a fire hydrant, a telephone pole, or some other obstruction and stage elaborate skateboard accidents, complete with "borrowed" lipstick for blood. One of us would stand aside wobbling a skateboard several feet off the ground so it appeared to be sailing through the frame.

Vienna boasted two swim clubs, each with its devoted membership: the older, Olympic-size Vienna Swim Club, located in the middle of Vienna Woods, and the smaller Vienna Aquatic Club, on Marshall Road near the intersection of Nutley Street. Our family belonged to the latter because it was nearer to our house on Dove Circle, but we kids often visited VSC as friends' guests or to attend parties.

I first heard the best band in Vienna, Us, at VAC. Their drummer was my local hero, Jeff Steele, with a lovely old Gretsch kit in Black Diamond Pearl; their skinny, precocious lead guitarist, Teddy Spelios, played the hell out of a Gretsch Country Gentleman just like George Harrison's (it looked even bigger on Teddy) and eventually ruined the finish by jamming his harmonicas between the bridge and the tailpiece; and their virtuoso bassist, Steve Gilles, would eventually join one of my own bands, the Cambridge Blue. The band Us was known for their authentic arrangements, but my main memory of them was of the night they were holding forth under the starlit suburban sky at VAC and Teddy flew into a rage when the club manager said the neighbors had demanded they turn down the volume. I *still* find myself siding with the neighbors whenever this subject comes up.

Both VSC and VAC were the sites of numerous teenage romances and pranks. My favorite of the latter was the time several of us broke into VAC late one night and I got the brilliant idea of diving off the high board—something I'd done a hundred times during daylight hours, not assessing the accompanying noises of rattling board and splashing water—thus announcing our presence and necessitating a hasty retreat in our soaked underwear as the authorities pursued us through woods infested with poison ivy.

The mid-Atlantic region enjoys a temperate climate

with four distinct seasons, each with its charms and irritations. Like most children, I loved snow and all its possibilities, especially the thrill of sledding at top speed down our hill. I experienced a frightening moment of claustrophobia one day inside a low igloo I had built a bit too solidly in the front yard. But of course I lost my enthusiasm for the white stuff when I began driving. Since we lived on a circle at the top of a hill—an arrangement that a Native American documentary filmmaker would one day tell me was considered the ideal community—the municipal snowplows generally made a bad situation worse when they took their cursory stab at our street. You'd spend half the day shoveling out your sidewalk and driveway and the other half extricating your just-freed car from the glacier the plows had left behind. Late one night years later, when a gig on which I was hired to play bass was canceled at the last minute because of an ice storm, I had to leave my car at the bottom of the hill and crawl home on my hands and knees, instrument slung onto my back. I developed a theory that the perfect year would be two weeks of light snow for Christmas followed immediately by eleven and a half months of summer.

Maple Avenue had firmly established itself as the main drag by the time I reached my teens, and our hangouts expanded accordingly. One of my favorites during the early fashion-conscious years was Normford's Style Shop, in the shopping center that featured the Giant supermarket. I loved the smell of the place as much as the clothes themselves. Another teen fave was Vienna Pizza, a tiny chrome-plated dive in another shopping center closer to the old section of town. We'd go to Vienna Pizza for weekend lunches and to play the jukebox. To this day, the songs "Like a Rolling Stone" and "Help!" evoke the smell of tomato sauce and the taste of root beer. The *original* shopping center on Maple Avenue, at the corner of Lawyers Road across from the Money & King Funeral Home, featured an old-time drugstore with a soda fountain, where I consumed many a sandwich and chocolate milkshake after my weekly drum lesson on Church Street.

In future decades Vienna would be home to several excellent ethnic restaurants: Afghan, Chinese, French, Greek, Indian, Italian, Japanese, Mexican, Turkish, and other cuisines were available many minutes closer to home than the parking hassles of Georgetown.

In 1967 Dad was appointed consul general to Amsterdam, and I embarked on the most memorable chapter of my youth. I returned to Virginia in 1969 for college, and my folks returned to the Dove Circle house, further degraded by careless tenants, in 1972. By then Vienna resembled any other town blighted by urban sprawl and had lost nearly all its charm for me. In 1989 I inherited the house, made it my own, and lived there more or less happily, give or take several feet of snow, until I escaped to Key West in 2000. The last lesson I learned there was never to sell a house to neurotic fair-weather friends. I haven't visited Vienna in nearly fifteen years and have no desire to see what else has become of the place.

Every generation treasures its version of the good old days, which for most of us comprise our carefree teens and early twenties. I feel immensely fortunate to have finished elementary school in Israel and high school in Holland—

college, back in the culturally illiterate U.S.A., was a bit of a letdown—but I remember "old" Vienna just as fondly. (More reminiscences appear in my book *The Human Drummer: Thoughts on the Life Percussive.*) Mostly I envy those pioneers' kids who knew the future nation's capital as a riverside oasis on the eastern edge of the New World.

OUT OF SEQUENCE

*S*yracuse, New York, native Freddie van Rijn was one of those people whose internal chemical electricity causes wristwatches and other mechanical objects to malfunction. Doctors had diagnosed Freddie's rare disorder in 1963, when he entered the seventh grade: the normally alert and energetic boy kept missing the school bus because his windup alarm clock failed to wake him. But Freddie had known since early childhood that his curse came with an astounding gift: telekinesis. Without lifting a finger, Freddie could cause toy trains to speed up and slow down, redirect deviously pitched softballs toward the sweet spot of his bat, steer the class bully's bicycle noisily into a cluster of aluminum trash cans, and perform other useful tasks. Once he began noticing girls, Freddie discovered he could charge the air around a particularly cute subject and cause her to look involuntarily into his eyes. Freddie did not expect normal people to understand his condition, which, excepting his doctors, he kept to himself. By his teens, Freddie had decided to use his powers only for good and had allowed all manner of clueless "heroes," nonprofit organizations, and government institutions to take credit for his anonymous contributions to society. In college, Freddie found that his disorder also affected early digital devices such as pocket calculators. His career choices narrowed to low-tech fields wherein he could cause minimal damage to office equipment. By the year 1989, when he finally bought one of the little Macintosh computers that were sweeping the nation, Freddie had learned that he could control certain telekinetic problems but that the occasional unpleasant surprise was always waiting around the corner. The computer was an amazing tool, provided Freddie could focus his thoughts; if his mind wandered, the screen would fill up with nonsense.

In the brutal winter of 2004, fifty-three-year-old Latin professor Freddie van Rijn was browsing in his local library when he came across a dog-eared American Automobile Association handbook to the subtropical island of Key West. Freddie looked out the window at the six-foot snowdrifts abutting the building and decided he deserved a vacation—but no way was he going to drive that distance when he had accrued only a two-week sabbatical. Recent improvements in air-traffic control systems assured telekinetic Freddie that he could fly, comfortable in the expectation that he and his fellow passengers would arrive intact and at the correct destination.

The first things Freddie did after checking into the Gardens Hotel at the corner of Angela and Simonton Streets were to hang his parka in the closet, remove all his clothes, and stretch out on the crisp white sheets. The breeze from the ceiling fan tickled Freddie's graying chest hair as he stared in amazement out the window at his own personal jungle. He got up, put on his trunks, went downstairs, jumped in the pool, enjoyed a rum and Coke at the poolside bar, exchanged pleasantries with a few fellow snowbirds, and booked a massage at a local spa. After supper at Antonia's, Freddie decided to stroll the main drag, Duval Street.

Freddie was immediately glad that he briefly had explored the quiet area surrounding his hotel before subjecting himself to the vulgar commercial sideshow that greeted him on Duval. He walked past one tacky establishment after another, amazed that anyone raised in the civilized world would enter such a place. The slow parade of slovenly tourists, aggressive street performers, and belligerent vagrants was equally disconcerting. He could not decide which was worse, the deafening, poorly performed music that poured out of nearly every doorway or the freezing draft of needless air-conditioning that wafted from open windows. Finally Freddie approached the reasonably sophisticated facade of La Te Da, a whitewashed bar on upper Duval.

Sid Borman had been performing his solo-guitar shtick in Key West for twenty years. He remembered when the local scene had boasted a number of decent bands and an equal number of venues willing to pay them something close to a living wage. These days, of course, bands per se were nearly nonexistent: the same dozen or so freelancers would regroup under different names and regurgitate their tired oldies for a transient audience that recycled itself every thirty minutes. Most regular local acts consisted of one or two singing musicians and a drum machine, often with a sequencer that provided whatever else was missing: bass, strings, horns, even vocal harmonies, all resembling the soundtrack to a science-fiction movie. As the economy had worsened, Sid himself had followed suit. The conservatory-bred musician prided himself on such an accurate sense of rhythm that he could play the unaccompanied introduction to a song knowing that when he tapped the pedal switch his drum machine and sequencer would kick in at precisely the correct tempo.

Five minutes after Freddie van Rijn took a seat at the La Te Da bar, Sid began one of his signature tunes, the Beatles' "Nowhere Man." Sid's uncanny *a cappella* John Lennon impression was harmonized by perfect digital replicas of Paul McCartney and George Harrison, raising nostalgic smiles throughout the room. When the "group" joined in, however, Ringo Starr's drum pattern sounded more like a polka than a medium rock beat, and the other virtual instruments were playing a completely different song in several keys at once. Sid aborted the tune as the audience laughed mercilessly. He always had relied on the standard soloist's joke for such a malfunction, which in his case was rare: "Gee, I guess I should pay my band more money."

Sid ignored an old drunk's loud comment, "*What fuckin' band?*" and checked his settings. Everything looked perfectly normal. After a brief apology, Sid restarted the song.

This time, however, even Paul and George had defected: the *a cappella* intro was a dissonant disaster, interrupted simultaneously by the drum part to Van Halen's "Jump," the keyboard backing to Don Henley's "Boys of Summer," and the bass line to "I'm Gonna Wash That Man Right Outa My Hair," from the musical *South Pacific.* Sid shut down all his gear, to general merriment on the part of listeners and staff, and hoped that a reboot would fix the situation. It did not, and a third brief musical depiction of a Manhattan traffic jam brought Sid's regular act to an unceremonious close. He spent the rest of the evening playing songs that required only one voice and one guitar played by a live human being.

Freddie van Rijn nursed his second rum and Coke of the day with a satisfied grin on his face for a few minutes and then decided to start making his way back down Duval toward his hotel. By the end of the night, those La Te Da listeners who had not fled the premises would fill Sid Borman's tip jar. Several patrons would remark to the bartender that they appreciated being able to hold a conversation without screaming their heads off.

Freddie passed other venues where similarly dismal one- and two-person acts were in place. He could not bring himself to enter, but he paused long enough in each doorway to cause a few more digital derailments. Patrons poured out en masse onto the sidewalk as bewildered musicians fiddled uselessly with their electronics and bar managers upbraided them for chasing away their lifeblood.

Freddie was enjoying himself so much by the time he reached Angela Street that he decided to descend all the way into the belly of the beast, just to see how bad it could get. At Duval and Caroline Streets he paused at the Bull & Whistle Bar to sabotage a fat little blonde wearing an electric guitar as a prop and lip-synching Joan Jett's "I Love Rock and Roll" to the accompaniment of a blaring CD player. Freddie waited to confirm that this supposedly was a professional act and not a drunken audience member performing karaoke. He walked on smiling as the CD skipped ahead several songs and the blonde stared accusingly at her dusty machine. By the time he crossed the cacophonous corner of Duval and Greene Streets, where a pair of musical comedians traded sophomoric obscenities from the stage of packed Sloppy Joe's, Freddie decided to take his concierge's advice and sample the best *mojito* in town, at El Meson de Pepe. On his way to the end of Duval, Freddie was encouraged by the illusion that a full band was playing at the Hog's Breath Saloon—only to discover that the band consisted of two young men (brothers, as it turned out), one of whom played guitar and sang; the other sang while playing the drums with his feet and right hand and grabbing at the frets of a bass guitar with his left hand. They were playing the Who's "Pinball Wizard," minus everything that Freddie had ever considered somewhat entertaining about the Who. He felt sufficiently sorry for this duo and left them to their labor.

The outdoor patio at El Meson de Pepe was also crowded, and Freddie was lucky to find a seat at the bar directly across from the stage. The band was on a break, but the presence on stage of actual instruments—guitar, flute, sax, vibes, congas, other percussion—gave Freddie hope. His transcendent *mojito* made him feel even more optimistic. Indeed, when the band began its second set, Freddie could do little more than tap his feet and nod his head in admiration for their authentic Afro-Cuban performances, supported by that fantastic offbeat bass line. But after a few tunes Freddie began to realize that even this trio was playing to tracks, albeit quite a bit more sophisticated than the tracks he had endured up the street. Their repertoire was so invigorating, as evidenced by the many accomplished dancers swaying and sweating on the brick courtyard, that Freddie did not have the heart to unleash his telekinetic powers. He ordered a second *mojito,* staggered back to the Gardens, and fell into a deep sleep. He dreamed of Leonard Bernstein leading the New York Philharmonic through the Symphonic Dances from *West Side Story.*

By the end of his first week in Key West, Freddie van Rijn had short-circuited so many local soloists and duos that the phenomenon inspired a front-page story in the *Key West Citizen.* Everyone from UFO experts at the local Naval Air Station to scientists at the National Oceanic and Atmospheric Administration weighed in with erudite explanations, and predictably lame jokes appeared in the *Citizen*'s anonymous "Citizen's Voice" column. One after another, local acts drove their cheesy gadgets to Miami for repairs and resumed performing music the old-fashioned way. No club owners' fortunes were flushed into the sea as a result. Listeners, musicians, and residents felt as if they were on to something new and refreshing.

The following Monday morning, Monroe County homicide detective and part-time professional drummer Rich Castillo was summoned to his boss's office. Sheriff Rick "Ace" Rothstein had heard about the strange goings-on in Key West's previously digitized music scene and was curious to learn what Lieutenant Castillo might know about it. Rothstein had good reason to single out Rich for questioning.

Rich and Rothstein got along fine, though Rich had never apologized to him or to anyone else for the musical moonlighting that occupied his weekends.

"Sit down, Rich," Rothstein drawled.

The detective smiled at his employer, wondering what piece of bloody evidence he could have overlooked in the months since the popular chief's reelection.

"I suppose that as a musician you've heard about these electric shenanigans going on among your buddies," Rothstein smiled.

Rich long ago had learned to overlook the layperson's ignorance of his avocation. The American school system simply had failed its citizens, and there was little Rich could do about it (though at that moment he was thinking that in 1965 *the Electric Shenanigans* would have been a good name for a band). "Yes," he smiled, "it's bizarre." Bizarre, yes; homicidal, no, at least not yet.

"And," Rothstein continued, "please forgive my asking you this, but I can't help wondering whether it could have anything to do with that inflammatory article you wrote earlier this year for *Solares Hill*."

Rich sat back, surprised that Rothstein even knew about the piece, and more surprised that rumors in Key West's uncontroversial arts community had crossed the big man's desk.

On June 3, 2004, *Solares Hill,* a now defunct weekly covering local culture and politics, had published an article entitled "Why All the Fake Music?" by Rich Castillo, drummer, lead singer, and founder of the Rich Castillo Band (formerly the Tropical Snobs). The piece had lamented the overabundance of prerecorded music on local stages and had promoted a return to "real" musicmaking. Not surprisingly, a number of hack musicians had attacked Castillo in the press for threatening their livelihoods.

Rich assured Rothstein that whereas he welcomed the sudden involuntary musical reform taking place around town, neither he nor anyone he knew had anything to do with it. The acoustic percussionist explained further that he lacked the expertise to sabotage a toaster, let alone a drum machine or a sequencer. The breakdowns were remarkable, and Rich was glad to look into it—again, off the clock, since his regular beat involved dead people, not fried circuit boards—but Rich was as baffled as anyone.

A week later, Freddie van Rijn returned home to Syracuse. Key West's drum machines and sequencers came back from Miami accompanied by technicians' notes saying they had found nothing wrong with them, the devices' owners resumed their former ways, the talk died down, and most people forgot all about the strange fortnight during which live music in Key West had sounded musical.

Typically, Freddie van Rijn's brief reign of terror produced an unexpected, if ephemeral, benefit. Rich Castillo had found the phenomenon sufficiently interesting to send copies of the local press to the *Miami Herald* and to the Miami office of the musicians' union. (Local 655, located actually in Fort Lauderdale, somehow expected to administer musical activities in Broward, Glades, Hendry, Indian River, Martin, Miami-Dade, Monroe [i.e., the Keys], Okeechobee, Palm Beach, and Saint Lucie counties, except the town of La Belle, which was in the jurisdiction of Local 427-721, located across the state in St. Petersburg.) The Miami local in turn forwarded the material to the head office in New York. This prompted the American Federation of Musicians to investigate reports of unethical, unfair, and in some cases illegal exploitation of musicians in Key West. For a day or two there even was some discussion of reestablishing a local office in the Southernmost City. As of the year 2014, however, the cash-strapped AFM, whose membership has declined steadily for the past decade, has had nothing more to say on the subject.

PERILS OF PARIS

For sixteen-year-old future concert pianist Gerald Gensler, the 1967-68 school term was a time of disruption, discovery, and, ultimately, dizzying love. In contrast to that turbulent time in American history, it also was what Gerald would recall as his slapstick period.

Gerald was one of several hundred young Americans enrolled at the International High School in Paris. His transplantation there from Alexandria, Virginia, because of his father's diplomatic career accounted for the disruption, the subsequent discoveries, and, after a semester of acclimation, a new girlfriend to replace the one back home without whom Gerald had promised he could not live.

In Old Town Alexandria, Gerald had adopted the "collegiate" style of dress peculiar to his social set (as distinguished from the sloppy, menacing attire of the "greasers"): a button-down long-sleeve oxford shirt in any of several acceptable colors or muted patterns; generally dark pleated dress trousers; black or cordovan penny loafers, alternating with brown laced wing tips; and a matching belt with a horseshoe-shaped brass buckle. In cool weather Gerald added a tasteful V-necked sweater; his favorite was a green cashmere item he had received as a birthday gift from his father's attractive young secretary, who said the sweater matched Gerald's hazel eyes. (The perky civil servant had stayed late after a particular cocktail party at the Gensler residence, taken Gerald aside in the library, and tipsily confessed her unrealizable crush on him; it would turn out that she was in fact sleeping with Gerald's dad.) It was not unusual to see Gerald walking the halls at school wearing an impeccably knotted tie and a tweed herringbone jacket for absolutely no reason. All his garments bore names chosen from a rigidly observed roster of permissible designers. By the end of his junior term in Paris, having endured a certain amount of good-natured ribbing from his new cosmopolitan classmates, Gerald had acceded to their more casual, less conformist look; but during that first semester Gerald seemed glad to resemble his male teachers.

One autumn afternoon Gerald was walking home in his heavy wing tips after buying school supplies downtown when he felt a sudden faint burning sensation in his left ankle. For a block or so he attributed this feeling to the stiff grownup shoes he did not particularly like but had bought because every other respectable guy in suburban D.C. had worn them. As Gerald continued down the busy Parisian sidewalk, the pain did not cease. Finally Gerald stepped out of the flow of pedestrian traffic and into a shop doorway. Lifting his stylish cuffs and looking down, he saw, to his astonishment, a tenpenny nail sticking out of his ankle between the bone and the Achilles tendon. The nail was embedded a good quarter of an inch into Gerald's skin. Somehow Gerald had managed to pick up the nail in the instep of his right shoe and kick it into his left ankle. There was no nearby construction or any other plausible explanation for the nail's presence on the sidewalk. To the self-conscious adolescent, the surreal sight caused more embarrassment than alarm; he quickly reached down, removed the nail, wiped away a small amount of blood from the tip, and put the nail in his right jacket pocket. (The nail did not appear rusty, but Gerald had heard about lockjaw and figured a second opinion might be in order.) Gerald stuck a finger down his fluffy black sock, observed the even smaller amount of blood that had oozed from the wound, and continued walking home. There he cleaned and dressed the little puncture and went upstairs to begin his homework.

At supper Gerald mentioned the minor miracle to his parents, both of whom had served in the army medical corps after World War II. As expected, Gerald's dad laughed off the incident, merely wondering aloud at the odds of such an occurrence. Mrs. Gensler, however, insisted on seeing the wound after supper and then suggested that Gerald stay home from school the next day and visit a doctor, just in case her son had acquired a life-threatening disease from the congested urban street.

As a young boy Gerald had suffered his share of ear infections, fevers, and other childhood ailments that required an antibiotic injection in the butt; he therefore had developed a general distrust of the medical establishment. He and his mom were relieved when the rumpled old French physician declared the injury was nothing and saw no need for the tetanus shot a stateside doctor probably would have prescribed. The wound healed in short order.

One afternoon about a week thereafter, Gerald was in the family garage helping his thirteen-year-old brother finish a project for shop class. Randall had been using a handsaw while kneeling on the floor behind his brother and had forgotten to hang it back on the wall. At some point Gerald stepped on the saw handle, causing the blade to flip up and scrape his left ankle about an inch above the spot where he had picked up the nail. The resultant cut, though not serious, looked reasonably ugly, and Gerald would wear a faint scar there for the rest of his life.

On an evening not long after that incident, Gerald and Randall were in the kitchen while their parents were away at an embassy function. Living temporarily in the gastronomical capital of the West had failed to cure the brothers of an occasional craving for unhealthy American food, and they decided to fry hamburgers using frozen patties their mom had bought at the army commissary. When two of the patties refused to separate under reasonable finger pressure, the teenagers decided to attack the problem with a long knife. For decades Gerald would recognize *that* scar, in the palm of his left hand, and would wonder whether it accounted in any way for the rudimentary cooking skills that plagued his relationships with women.

Gerald had always been a good sprinter, and one morning later in the fall semester he accepted a friend's challenge to a fifty-yard race down an unfinished gravel roadbed. Gerald took the lead immediately and felt confident of winning, but just to be sure he increased his speed toward the finish line. He was leaning so far ahead that he hurtled over the line and had to break his fall onto the gravel with his hands. The several nasty little scars he earned as a result of this rare competitive impulse would sometimes remind him of the opening scene of *A Hard*

Day's Night, where George Harrison and Ringo Starr tumble painfully to the sidewalk as they and their mates outrun the crowd of screaming girls.

A similar event took place during a volleyball game in the school gym just before the winter break. Gerald and a teammate knocked heads so violently in pursuit of the ball that Gerald fell to the floor unconscious. For several seconds everyone gathered around him as he woke smarting and needing to throw up. The coach informed Gerald that he had suffered a mild concussion, and the kids went about the rest of their day. (This was some years before every schoolyard mishap triggered an automatic lawsuit.)

As a musician Gerald loved all branches of the performing arts and participated however and whenever he could. Since the chorus teacher was slated to play the piano for the spring musical, Gerald volunteered instead to serve on the stage crew. One afternoon backstage during rehearsals, Gerald was carrying an armload of props to their onstage locations as a fellow crewmember followed close behind him carrying a tall ladder. Not watching where he was going, the other kid dislodged the glass globe of an overhead light fixture. The globe fell from the high ceiling and struck Gerald right on the top of his head, raining shattered glass all around him. Gerald shut his eyes instinctively, but a shard grazed his chin. The clean cut healed quickly, leaving a small but visible scar. This manly disfiguration would one day add a rugged note to the classical artist's publicity photographs.

Toward twilight on an early summer's day about a week after school ended, Gerald and his new girlfriend,

Kelly, were humoring her obnoxious eight-year-old brother, Carey, with a game of hide-and-seek in a big park. The area where the kids were playing included a grassy clearing about half the circumference of a baseball diamond surrounded by thick woods. The kids did not know that one of the wooded paths intersected a horse trail delineated by a barbed-wire fence. At one point in his search for Carey, Gerald took off running down the shaded path and ran straight into the invisible fence. Fortunately Gerald was too short to hit the higher of two strands of wire; but his right thigh struck the lower strand with such force that he flipped over it and landed with his palms in the dirt of the trail. There Gerald hung upside down for many long seconds as Kelly and Carey, the latter having emerged from his nearby hiding spot, laughed uncontrollably in the background. Gerald righted himself just as two adult riders galloped past inches away, unaware of the clumsy American's presence. Stepping back from the wire, Gerald discovered a two-inch rip in the leg of his brown corduroy jeans; the corresponding gash underneath was bleeding profusely. Gerald blotted the mess with his right hand as the snickering trio made their way in the gathering darkness back to Kelly's house.

Typically, Kelly's dad dismissed the injury (though he later agreed with Mr. Gensler that his son seemed just a bit accident-prone), and her mom insisted that they take Gerald immediately to the emergency room. There, another disheveled French doctor dressed the jagged wound, saw no need for stitches, and sent Gerald on his way. This most impressive of Gerald's battle scars would provide the occasional paragraph of pillow talk long after

Kelly and her family had disappeared from Gerald's life.

Pianist Gerald Gensler remains one of the few people he knows who have never broken a bone, a happy condition he attributes partly to his distaste for snow: during Gerald's three years in Paris, an equal number of his classmates had returned from Alpine skiing holidays with one or more limbs encased in plaster. This memory sometimes amuses Gerald as he glances at his hands between movements of some particularly difficult concerto.

PIANO TRIO

Carmen and I played together in the college jazz band. She was a voluptuous blonde, not my type. But she was flirtatious, and I was curious about her nimble pianist's fingers. We propositioned each other one evening after rehearsal.

Our one-night stand was notable mainly for its distractions. Carmen had a room on the second floor of an old woman's house. This was a conservative small town, and Carmen's landlady might not have taken kindly to the presence of a late-night guest. As it turned out, I do not see how we could have been more obvious.

We were quiet enough about slipping in through the side door and up the stairs.

Carmen was having last-minute jitters about our encounter. She spent forever in the bathroom and made a rather embarrassing wedding-night show of emerging in a long sheer negligee, *Be gentle with me* glowing on her studied pout. (The girl was no virgin.) Then we climbed into her single bed.

Bad idea. We should have chosen the floor, a chair, or anything else. This was the noisiest bed since the invention of steel. Just pressing on it was funny, and I knew it would take intense concentration to block out the clattering rhythms to come. Carmen suggested we turn on the television. This, of course, only deepened the comic effect. In a few minutes we were fucking wildly, the bed evoking the image of some psychotic percussion ensemble conducted by Johnny Carson, while a blissful Carmen purred, "Ooh, it feels so good."

I hope the old Baptist downstairs enjoyed it half as much as we did, the next time we showed up for rehearsal.

SAVED BY THE GUITAR SOLO

One slow afternoon in 1995, during his days as the jazz buyer of a large Baltimore record store, Isaac "Ike" Ireton found himself pondering one of life's mysteries: popular songs whose most attractive feature is their guitar solo.

Two specific examples came immediately to Ike's mind, remarkable especially for the fact that the songs in question were recorded by pop groups Ike would not have crossed the street to hear in concert: Tommy James & the Shondells and Bad Company. The two songs, both ballads, were "Crimson and Clover" and "Feel Like Makin' Love."

The Shondells' lame attempt at psychedelia, complete with some of the most distasteful use of the wah-wah pedal ever committed to vinyl, was every bit as hokey as that group's previous hits, wending its way one saccharine measure after another, until suddenly the clouds parted and a gorgeous little riff, played by Ed Gray on a steel guitar, appeared several times between repetitions of the song's signature "power chords." That the steel guitar showed up here out of the blue despite its nearly stigmatic association with country music was remarkable enough (the instrument's Hawaiian connection is older and less familiar); that this riff lifted the song out of its bathos for a few bars was a gift from studio heaven.

Bad Company certainly was a more powerful musical

force than the Shondells, but nothing in the band's repertoire had ever caught Ike's attention until the evening during grad school when he was driving home through rush-hour traffic and "Feel Like Makin' Love" came on the radio. The easygoing groove and sleepily masculine vocals, reminding Ike a bit of the Band (he even conjectured that the song might have been an "homage" to "The Weight"), were attractive, if not compelling. Again, however, when the verses and choruses made way for Mick Ralphs's guitar solo, all was understood: the simplest possible motif, harmonized and played twice in exact repetition, absolutely made the song.

Crunchier still was the epically overplayed and parodied "Stairway to Heaven," by Bad Company's sponsor, the insufferable Led Zeppelin. This brontosaurus of a band topped Ike's list of the three ugliest-sounding groups of all time, the other two being Queen and Rush. Ike respected John Bonham's swinging rock drumming, but he could not endure Robert Plant's caterwauling or Jimmy Page's tendency to rush the beat—a common affliction among rock guitarists. (John Paul Jones was the group's reserved secret weapon, à la John Entwistle, the brilliant bassist of a sloppy garage band called the Who.) The merciful arrival of Page's solo on "Stairway" provided as good an example as any of actual music by what younger listeners call the greatest rock band in history.

Ike considered this phenomenon and tried to think of other entries. Mostly he came up with perfectly fine songs whose memorable guitar solos engaged the listener as assuredly as the songs' harmony, melody, rhythm, and lyrics: Badfinger's "Day after Day" (played and produced by George Harrison); the Beatles' "And Your Bird Can Sing," "Another Girl," "The End," "Every Little Thing," "Fixing a Hole," "A Hard Day's Night," "I'm Only Sleeping," "Maxwell's Silver Hammer," "Michelle," "The Night Before," "Nowhere Man," "Octopus's Garden," "Roll Over, Beethoven," "She's a Woman," "Something," "Taxman," "While My Guitar Gently Weeps," "You're Going to Lose That Girl," and many more; the Beau Brummels' "Just a Little"; Chuck Berry's "Johnny B. Goode"; Boston's "More than a Feeling"; Lindsey Buckingham's minimalist "Go Your Own Way" with Fleetwood Mac and virtuosic "Countdown" as a solo artist; the Byrds' "Eight Miles High" (an overreaching tribute to John Coltrane), "I'll Feel a Whole Lot Better," and "Turn! Turn! Turn!"; Cream's "Crossroads" and many other singable improvisations by Eric Clapton; Crosby, Stills, Nash & Young's "Teach Your Children" (with pedal steel played by the self-taught Jerry Garcia); numerous reckless flamenco flourishes by the Doors' Robby Krieger; the Eagles' "One of These Nights"; Bill Haley's "Rock around the Clock"; all the solos on George Harrison's *All Things Must Pass,* the most famous of which were played by George's pal Eric; too many Jimi Hendrix solos to mention; Allan Holdsworth's "Fred," "Wildlife," and other breaths of fresh air from the smog of jazz-rock fusion; Buddy Holly's "Peggy Sue"; Jefferson Airplane's "Somebody to Love"; the Kinks' adolescent "You Really Got Me"; the Lovin' Spoonful's "Do You Believe in Magic"; the Moody Blues' "New Horizons" and "Ride My See-Saw"; the Police's "King of Pain"; Linda Ronstadt's "Justine" (a no-nonsense essay for *bass* guitar); the Yardbirds' "Shapes of Things," along with practically every other utterance by the amazing Jeff Beck; and the Youngbloods' "Get Together."

Ike Ireton's main instrument was the saxophone— soprano, alto, tenor, baritone—and he doubled generously on flute. Ike had taken up his second instrument, the drums, mostly for fun, though this versatility yielded a lucrative sideline. Like many other passengers aboard Starship Earth, however, Ike could occasionally be seen accompanying his radio with hormonal episodes of air guitar that seemed to satisfy some universal human itch. Ike envied all those guitar heroes, even the ones whose busy solos had managed to ruin otherwise decent songs (too many examples of which will live for all time alongside the abovementioned exceptions), because at least those overachievers were devoted to their craft.

As an approaching store customer prepared to shatter Ike's reverie, he raised an imaginary champagne flute to Leo Fender, Orville Gibson, Friedrich Gretsch, Christian Frederick Martin, Adolph Rickenbacker, and their disciples.

SCARRED FOR LIFE

About eleven o'clock on the morning of July 3, 1967, Kathy McNeil, aged nine, was crossing the manicured lawn between two sections of the Baltimore apartment complex where she lived with her eight-year-old brother and their single mother when Kathy saw something she would never forget.

She passed there almost daily on her way to the school bus or, in summer, to meet with friends who lived in one or another of the units in the tightknit suburban community. Her mom, who in childhood and in marriage had lived in detached homes in nicer parts of town, had told Kathy that apartment complexes often housed unsophisticated, undesirable characters who should be ignored, avoided, or reported to the authorities. Kathy understood this warning vaguely and filed it in her consciousness along with numerous other mysterious things her mother had said that Kathy realized were intended to keep her safe. Kathy's mother was all the adult family she had.

What Kathy saw that morning as she passed a row of ground-floor apartments made her stop and wonder. At the sliding screen door off one of the identical patios to her left was a young man with no clothes on. He stood in the doorway casually as if awaiting a taxi or considering some grown-up problem; he seemed unaware of her presence or of the fact that he was naked. To Kathy he could have been

167

anywhere from twenty to forty years old; he was in fact sixteen. He had brown hair on his head and a lesser amount of wispy brown fuzz on his chest. It took Kathy a moment to notice the corresponding halo surrounding his private parts because his thing was sticking straight up. The long pink shaft looked like a featherless bird or some sort of jungle creature, a chameleon, perhaps; its upright attitude appeared to Kathy as a miracle. Kathy had seen her brother's penis, had asked her mom about it and received more vague, unintelligible information, and had added that explanation to her growing collection of useless data—but she had never seen the thing perform any sort of trick. Brian's little knob looked simply like a protruding version of the little knob at the top of her slit, and Kathy accepted this enigma as she accepted the fact that her mother was taller than she and had two bumps on her chest where she herself had only two little berries like Brian's.

Kathy stood staring at the young man and his upright lizard-thing. The totem seemed to offer her a message, some clue to human existence.

Suddenly the guy noticed her presence. He smiled and said, "Hi."

The combination of the unprecedented sight and the man's friendly greeting startled her; but Kathy found herself frozen in place, as if she had stepped into thick mud. She could offer no reply.

As abruptly as the man had said hello, his face became serious and he said, "Oh, my. Pardon me," in a funny, formal voice. Then he stepped back from the doorway and disappeared.

Kathy remained in place for a moment. The few times she had seen her mother undressed had been clouded in embarrassment and quick motions to grab a towel or a robe; similarly, her brother's rare nakedness had been explained away as a minor intrusion. Kathy felt sad that the affable young man had retreated from the doorway. Whereas Brian's cute peanut had been merely different, the man's alert birdlike appendage was interesting, perhaps a bit beautiful.

After a few moments, Kathy remembered that her mom had sent her on an errand to borrow a half-pint of whipping cream from a neighbor. She completed her mission and returned the way she had come. When she passed the young man's patio, the glass door had been closed and the curtain drawn.

Based on her mother's warnings about strangers, Kathy knew she should report the incident. When she did, Mrs. McNeil flew into a rage. Kathy compared the young man's strange beauty with her mom's anger and realized something was not right; about which thing she was not sure. She could tell that she herself should be offended by the man's nakedness, but all she really felt was confused curiosity. She knew from tattling on Brian over the years that the man was in some sort of trouble, but she wished suddenly that she had kept the matter to herself. Kathy had the sense that any real danger lay not in the man's presence in the doorway but in her mother's reaction.

Mrs. McNeil made Kathy take her to the spot and point out the door. When they arrived, the curtain was still drawn but the sliding glass door was open. The air was warm but pleasantly dry for midsummer. After standing at the edge of the patio for a few moments, Mrs. McNeil said loudly, "If you're in there, you'd better show yourself right quick. I'm calling the cops."

The curtain fluttered slightly in the breeze.

About ten minutes later, a young police officer knocked on the man's door. He was surprised to see a teenage boy answer it, wearing expensive leather sandals, pressed khaki shorts, and a white soccer jersey with a green number 69 printed on it. The patrolman told the boy that they needed to talk and invited himself in. The two sat opposite each other in the living room, the cop explained the situation and said that children rarely lie about such things, and he encouraged the young man to admit his crime. "This little girl may never trust a man again," he said. "She may be scarred for life." As he sat assessing the nervous subject and his posh British accent, the policeman felt instinctively that the boy was harmless. Still, the cop represented the community and had a job to do. He did not buy the teen's steadfast denial of the event and hoped he could get him to acknowledge his offense without causing undue trauma to him, the girl, or the mother. At the end of the interview, he told sixteen-year-old Trevor Knightsbridge he was under arrest and took him to the local police station. There was no need for handcuffs. Trevor was pleasant, cooperative, and surprisingly calm. The cop assumed this demeanor reflected shock and disbelief combined with upper-class reserve, or perhaps an overdose of unrealistic American television.

At the station the two were joined by an avuncular detective who entered the room carrying three cold bottles of Coca-Cola. He sat at his desk and smiled. After repeating the information he had been given, he grinned at the teenager and said, "You might be surprised to learn this, but I know exactly what your *69* T-shirt means. You're sixteen. You think about sex all the time, whether you know it or not. You're proud of your body, and since puberty you probably haven't shown it to anyone except in secret. I'll bet none of your girlfriends has ever seen you completely naked, right?"

Trevor sat silently trying to mask his mortification. The number on his shirt was actually a winking reference to his anticipated graduation year.

"Girls have touched you in the dark, and you've touched them, right?"

More silence.

"But this has all been sneaking around in cars and theaters and living rooms with parents upstairs, and you've never really been undressed with a girl, right?"

"Right," Trevor said finally, almost inaudibly.

"And so this morning, standing nude at that doorway, you got kind of a thrill when a pretty girl walked by, right?"

Trevor said nothing but seemed about to nod. His smile suggested he still hoped to get out of this.

"And frankly, I doubt any major injury was done. But her mom, or, as you probably would say, her *mum,* is furious. Civilized society does not accept this sort of behavior. Do you understand that?"

"Yes, sir," Trevor said quietly. He had heard the United States called by many names; *civilized* was not among them.

The detective and the patrolman sat smiling at Trevor,

who shifted in his seat.

"So, do you have anything to say about this situation?"

After a long silence, Trevor leaned forward and, his voice breaking, whispered, "I am sorry. It was an accident."

The detective sat back in his chair. "An accident?"

"A misunderstanding. That is to say, I didn't mean for anyone to see me," Trevor said, almost sobbing.

The cops viewed him with gentle skepticism.

"I sort of forgot where I was," he continued.

The detective took a sip of his Coke. "Well," he said, belching quietly to lighten the mood, "you were standing naked in a doorway that opened onto a public space."

Trevor drew himself upright in his chair. "Yes, but I was thinking of someone I know back home and totally lost track of time and place. I swear to you, before God, I had no idea anyone could see me through the screen door. I couldn't see into anyone else's flat across the lawn."

The cops looked at each other.

"That may be," the detective replied, "but this little girl was standing ten feet away and could see you quite clearly."

Trevor looked down. "I'm terribly sorry," he repeated.

The detective smiled. "I wish, and I'm sure you wish, that this *misunderstanding* could just go away. But your behavior has consequences. The girl's mother is adamant and wants to press charges. I'm afraid there's nothing I can do but refer this matter to the juvenile court system."

Trevor blanched. "What does that mean, exactly?"

"What that means," the detective continued, "is that you'll be charged with indecent exposure and that there will be a trial."

Trevor's eyes welled with tears.

"Now, I don't expect this to go any further than a stern warning from the judge and a meeting with a counselor," said the older man. "But you'd better prepare yourself for an unpleasant few days."

It turned out that Trevor Knightsbridge was an honors exchange student from London, visiting a local family while studying American literature at a summer program for gifted teens. Trevor's father was a member of the House of Commons and his mother a respected English playwright. They in turn were hosting Marla Blankenship, the teenage daughter of the family with whom Trevor was boarding. The Blankenships were renting temporarily because they had sold their house and the newly built one was not finished.

When the police explained the situation to Robert and Gail Blankenship, they reacted quietly and said they hoped the legal machinery could run its course without involving the high-profile London family.

On the day of the trial, Trevor, accompanied by his host parents, arrived wearing the single dark suit he had brought and had hoped not to need during his summer in casual America. As they stood waiting in the hallway outside the courtroom, Kathy McNeil and her mother got off the elevator.

Mrs. McNeil immediately placed her arm around Kathy and pulled her to her ample breast, glaring at Trevor with unvarnished disgust. Trevor and the Blankenships took a step backward.

Trevor could not help smiling apologetically at Kathy,

who could not help smiling apologetically at him.

No one said a word, and the two groups took up positions at opposite ends of the foyer. When the bailiff called them in, they entered the small courtroom in silence.

The trial lasted about fifteen minutes. The patrolman and the judge did nearly all the talking: the former repeating what had happened at the apartment and what had been said at the police station, the latter scolding Trevor for Mrs. McNeil's benefit and issuing the predicted order for counseling. Kathy and her mother exited the courtroom immediately thereafter. Trevor, his embarrassed guardians, and the cop hung back and left by another door.

At the single counseling session in a small courthouse office the following week, Trevor again repented his carelessness.

Smiling compassionately, the young female therapist concluded by saying, "I think we can assume that this will never happen again."

Trevor answered in the affirmative. By tacit agreement, he and Mr. and Mrs. Blankenship dropped the subject forever.

In 1976, after her mother had remarried and the new family had moved into a beautiful house near the Walters Art Museum, Kathy McNeil graduated *summa cum laude* from a cloistered private school and entered Johns Hopkins University with a major in psychology. She was the only virgin in her dormitory suite and the only girl in the building who had never been touched intimately. When asked about her inexperience, Kathy told her roommates she simply was waiting to meet the right boy.

"We call them *men* now," said Clarice Jensen, the freshman biology lab partner who was already annoying Kathy with her affectation that high school was years ago.

"Still," Kathy insisted, "I'm in no hurry."

Premed student Valerie Knowles hoped that Kathy's patience indicated latent lesbian tendencies. When one evening she made a stoned pass at Kathy, however, Val was disappointed.

In her sophomore year, Kathy McNeil met and fell in love with a Welsh history major named Trevor Thomas. In one semester she learned everything her freshmen roommates had hoped in one way or another to teach her. Her favorite feature of Trevor's lovemaking was his skillfully delayed climax, during which she felt free to whisper his name over and over again. The following term, having begun privately referring to her intellectually dull first boyfriend as *Tedious* Thomas, she met and fell in love with a Scottish music major named Trevor McGregor. After the young man's devotion to his violin started making Kathy feel like an unsympathetic accompanist, she met and fell in love with an Irish English major named Trevor Bloom. They stayed together through graduate school and were married aboard a schooner moored at the Inner Harbor. Three years later Kathy gave birth to their only child, Trevor Junior.

In 1997, as unmentioned thanks for not having reported his teenage misstep to his now deceased parents, the award-winning British novelist Trevor Knightsbridge sent Robert and Gail Blankenship a signed copy of his recently optioned political thriller *Scarred for Life,* along with an autographed head shot of actor Tom Cruise. Trevor soon would learn that his former American hosts had also died and that their daughter had inherited their home. In her thank-you letter, Marla Blankenship told Trevor Knightsbridge that she loved his book and could not wait to see the film. She said that if he was ever again in Baltimore he must pay her a visit.

THE SCULPTURE GARDENER

From a tape transcript found in the office of a recently deceased Key West psychiatrist

First of all, let's get one thing straight: I didn't move to Key West just for the weather, the water, the casual lifestyle, or the dubious pleasure of hearing potbellied old hippies play bad versions of Jimmy Buffett songs. OK, the weather was a major factor; I was sick of freezing this pretty little ass off in New York. And the brilliant light that shines on a tropical island is quite a refreshing contrast to the dreary concrete canyon I grew up in. But I moved here mainly for a job in the small but energetic local arts community. For years I'd crashed around various impoverished Manhattan nonprofits and, ready for a change, won a phone interview to take over a struggling noncommercial Key West gallery. This was almost fifteen years ago. I was prepared for the scary, grant-dependent pay at an arts agency but somewhat naive when it came to the high cost of living on this rock. Almost immediately on arriving here I found myself seeking a discreet way to supplement my income.

I've always looked good, and I've never apologized for the doors, literal and otherwise, that have opened for me as a result. Homecoming queen, "most popular" girl, first-chair flutist in Band despite being the second-best player, all the usual bullshit, long after which I took for granted the nervous advances of guys of all ages, whose sometimes adorable stammering would worsen the minute they learned I had a master's in arts administration, whatever that was. Down here, of course, it's *girls* of all ages too, and I'm pretty open-minded. Sex is sex, the way art is art: good, bad, indifferent, I usually can find something to like in everyone. My first New York employers made sure to bring me along whenever they were pitching the CEO of some arts-friendly corporation; back at the office, we'd laugh at how easy it is to solicit large sums of money from horny millionaires of both genders when there's a hot babe in the room. Half the time I didn't even need to open my mouth. To speak, that is.

Which brings me to that sudden need for a discreet form of moonlighting. One evening my assistant and I were having dinner at a well-known Old Town restaurant when we overheard these four thirtyish guys at the next table, obviously tourists, comparing notes on a local escort service. Their consensus was that prostitution in Key West was much more expensive than back home. Never in a million years would I have considered that line of work until I heard how much money these idiots had wasted on what sounded like perfunctory sex.

The next afternoon I opened the phone book and started combing the escort agencies. Placing the calls was less embarrassing than the discovery that several different phone numbers pointed to the same few entrepreneurs, and I had to apologize more than once for repeating myself. But of course I landed half a dozen interviews, each of which resulted in a guaranteed offer. I had to "audition" for a couple of pretty gross men and one woman of a certain age whom I'll call Sally, but I kept my eyes on the prize. My original goal of discretion had run smack up against the possibility of erasing all my debt practically overnight.

Sally assured me I was entirely within my rights to refuse any activity I found objectionable. There isn't much I haven't done at least once—a threesome can be fun, with the right couple—but I draw the line at anal. *Yuck.* Some avenues are one-way for a good reason.

Fortunately I happened to be standing in Sally's office a few days later when the guy who would be my first client called. I'd shown up looking tastefully sexy—these days it's hard to tell a hooker from your average spring-breaker when it comes to evening wear—and was having minor doubts about this enterprise when I glanced at Sally's caller ID. The guy on the other end of the line was a prominent Key West sculptor who sat on our board of directors. I was still relatively new in town, but I thought there was no way he'd fail to recognize me. On the other hand, he was in great shape—by far the best-looking board member I'd ever seen—had written respected books on art history, and was quite wealthy (from his art or from another source, I wasn't sure). As Sally sat there covering the phone and awaiting my response, I compared my present salary with Sally's estimate of what I could earn in a year from her agency alone and decided then and there to quit the gallery. Having read about more than a few disgraced Key Westers who'd reinvented themselves with nary a blemish, I figured I could someday resurface in the legit world with enough money in the bank to be choosy. I mean, the two most visible members of the city commission are a blues-loving grocer and a strip-club owner, the town's most famous annual event involves people walking naked down the main drag, and *Cayo Hueso* made its original fortune looting shipwrecks. This ain't your normal fishing village. I told Sally I'd take the gig. It was eleven o'clock in the morning.

Examples of this guy's sculpture appeared all over town and in various cities around the world. Most of it was whimsical human figures in metal, often life-sized, usually heavy and industrial with lots of rust and rough edges. The pieces I'd seen in galleries and rich folks' courtyards blended beautifully with the Caribbean themes, tropical landscaping, and cheerful architecture that give Key West its unique charm—and they hardly prepared me for the examples I'd encounter in the artist's own yard.

It turned out he lived up the Keys a few miles, in a posh neighborhood where everyone had surrounded their overpriced stilt houses with lush greenery. The first thing I saw when I got out of the car was a pair of unpainted steel lovers fucking on the front lawn; on closer inspection the amorous duo revealed itself as a squeaky rocking bench. Reaching up to the sky between two coconut palm trees was a brightly polished chrome-plated nude with a huge erection that doubled as the hook on which the sculptor coiled his garden hose. Centered in a circle of royal palms was a bronze woman on her knees with her standing lover's entire cock in her mouth; verdigris ran down her face and neck like so much seminal overflow. I assumed similar pieces adorned parts of the property I couldn't see, but I'd wait for a guided tour. Smiling, I mounted the stairs.

The screen door was propped open, but the main door was closed; I was about to learn why. When the door opened, the local hero stood before me stark naked and hard as a rock. His erection wasn't quite as impressive as his chrome lawn boy's, but it was pretty nice: about seven inches long, thick, and smooth, with a useful upward curve. Except for the lightly graying sandy hair on his head, he was shaved from top to bottom. Combined with his powerful physique, the artist's hairless torso gave him a boyish charm.

"Glad to see me?" I smiled. I looked deep into his sparkling blue eyes and awaited the flustered shock of recognition.

Instead he merely flexed his cock and motioned me inside. "Absolutely," he answered.

The sculptor stepped aside, affording me a profile of his tight bod. As I entered the living room I realized his hard-on wasn't only for me: in the corner was a huge flat-screen TV on which an X-rated film was playing with the sound turned off. He had covered the brown leather sofa with beach towels and invited me to join him there. As Sally had instructed me, I requested that we take care of business first. The guy reached down to an end table, picked up the short stack of twenties, and handed them to me; slipping them into my purse wasn't as simple as it should've been, with that lovely penis pointing up at me from a foot away. A brief glance revealed that a drop of pre-come had already appeared.

"If you'll show me to your powder room," I said, "I'll join you in a minute." The bathroom on this floor was just on the other side of an oak spiral staircase. I went in, closed the door, washed my hands, and undressed. A guy who answers his door naked must like to get right to the point. Stripteasing and mutual disrobing could wait for a future visit, assuming I won his repeat business. I kept on my black heels.

When I returned to the living room, the sculptor was occupying the left third of the sofa, lightly touching himself and watching the TV screen. His cock jumped again when he turned to see that a good-looking naked woman had entered the room. I stood before him without blocking the screen so he could enjoy fantasy and reality simultaneously, and so he could confirm that, physically, at least, his money had been well spent. I assumed he would appreciate my own hairless condition, which for several years I'd maintained with a combination of shaving, waxing, laser treatments, and lots of moisturizer.

"Mother of God, you're beautiful," he smiled, still stroking his long shaft with slender, androgynous fingers.

I guessed he wore work gloves to create his jagged sculptures.

"Turn around, please," he said.

I did a slow three-sixty.

"I'd love for you to model for me sometime."

"I'd be honored," I replied, sitting beside him. I pointed to his cock and then to the TV. "Is this what you have in mind?" I wasn't sure what I'd meant by that, but I was beginning to think the guy was just an exhibitionist and wanted me to sit there watching him jack off. But he could've done that in town for half the money.

He took his hand away and patted my left forearm.

"Oh, no, dear, this is just an appetizer."

I sat back and watched the film for a moment. That's how long it took to realize it was a random compilation of facial come shots, one after the other, involving girls and guys of all varieties, the only common element being the obligatory huge cock. Some of the women were equally busty, but many had small or even tiny breasts. All the men were shown from the neck down; each could've been anyone. "Seriously, sweetie," I said, "what would you like to do?"

The sculptor picked up the remote and froze the frame in midstream. He set down the device and looked me over. "First," he said, "I'd like you to sit there and enjoy this cinematic masterpiece while I make you come."

I smiled appreciatively. Not what I'd expected from a client, especially my first. I leaned back and spread my legs.

He took up the remote and resumed the film. Then, instead of reaching over with his hands, he rose, placed a pillow on the floor between my feet, knelt, and went down on me as expertly as anyone I'd ever known.

"Oh my God!" I sighed. "This isn't what I was ex—"

"Shush," he whispered.

I obeyed. A few minutes later, I added: "I must warn you that I've been known to squirt when feeling particularly happy."

He paused and smiled up at me. "Nothing would make me happier myself," he said.

The endless parade of come shots was a bit much—I should think you'd become inured to them after a while— but what he was doing was heavenly. I closed my eyes most of the time, checking out the action now and then in case he knew the damn movie by heart and was about to quiz me. In another minute, I wouldn't have cared if he demanded I name all the state capitals in alphabetical order. He reached up and lightly pinched my nipples just as I came all over his face.

He reacted like the perfect gentleman he seemed, first impression notwithstanding. He knew precisely when to stop stimulating me. Laughing gently, he cupped one hand warmly over my vagina and with the other reached for the expensive hand towel folded on the end table. "That was lovely," he said, tending first to my wet thighs and then to his face.

"You're telling me!" I replied. I was still pulsating under his palm. "Wow. Thank you."

"You're most welcome. Just relax a moment. Would you like something to drink?"

It was still midday, but it also was Saturday. "What are you having?"

He sat back on the floor, his gorgeous hard-on commanding my attention. He crossed his ankles and interlocked his fingers around his knees. "Well, there's cold spring water, orange juice, *good* beer, wine—red or white—and rum."

I was almost tempted to ask him to brew a pot of coffee, just to watch him move around his kitchen for a while with that thing sticking up. And I hadn't had a chance to check out his butt. "Oh, let's have wine, your choice."

He rose and walked to the kitchen. *Great* ass. I got up and followed him. He opened the fridge and uncorked an opened bottle of pino grigio. He reached into a cabinet, brought down two sleek glasses, and poured. He handed one to me and lifted his. "To a memorable afternoon," he smiled.

I clicked his glass and sipped.

"Shall we go upstairs?" he asked.

"Your wish is my come-mand," I pronounced, feeling suddenly cheap.

His nonverbal response eased my embarrassment. Then: "There'll be no commands here, my love," he smiled, "unless you like that sort of thing."

I'd always found S and M to be somewhere between silly and insulting. "So far, we seem to like the same things. You lead the way." I would've volunteered to go first, but I enjoyed observing and teasing him.

He took my hand and led me up the spiral stairs.

His bedroom afforded a beautiful view of the yard through sliding glass doors that opened onto a small balcony. He or his predecessor must've lived there at least a decade; the trees were tall and full. In addition to palms there were ancient buttonwoods, a flaming royal poinciana, two cream-yellow frangipani, a fruit-bearing mango, sea grapes, purple-plumed scheffleras, a Barbados cherry, Jamaican dogwoods, and species I couldn't name. You could stand naked at the windows without seeing a single neighbor's house.

He stood behind me at a distance, admiring my figure.

I turned around. The king-size bed was in the middle of the room, with a full-length wall mirror on one side and the tall mirror of his dresser on the other. No mirror on the ceiling, but this was one visual guy. I watched him draw down the purple comforter. The fresh black satin sheets and pillowcases looked a bit Hugh Hefner, but I imagined they'd feel nice—and they'd probably been chosen to show off whatever sperm would manage to overshoot its intended target. He reclined on his side of the bed and patted the mattress on mine.

I felt so comfortable with my sculptor that I was afraid of violating a cardinal rule of this trade: no kissing on the lips. It's too emotional, too much like a normal love affair. Staying businesslike also enhances the naughty factor. I sat on the edge of the bed before twirling around and reclining at his side. "What's next?" I asked. "Would you like a little massage?"

"That would be wonderful," he smiled. He turned toward me and, before rolling onto his stomach, pushed his erection down between his legs.

"Ouch, doesn't that hurt?" I asked.

"It hurts more if I lie on it," he answered.

I didn't complain about the persistent distraction. I mounted his butt and began massaging his head, neck, and shoulders. When I moved down to squeeze those nice glutes and his legs, that thing hadn't softened a bit. I spun around to administer a brief foot rub. "Would you like to turn over now?" I asked, staying on my hands and knees so he'd have a nice view when he resumed his former position.

As he did, his heavy penis flipped up and smacked his abdomen loudly. We both giggled. As I tended to his feet, legs, chest, neck, and face, he gently touched me everywhere he could reach. I was enjoying my first appointment, reminding myself that a steady diet of nice guys was unlikely.

Next I lay at his side twirling my fingers through his hair. "Would you like me to touch you now?" I asked. "Or would you prefer my mouth or—"

"I'd like a little of everything, if that's all right," he smiled dreamily.

I reached down and gently encased his tight balls in my fingertips. His cock throbbed. I caressed the balls for a while and then traveled ever so slowly up the silky shaft to the tip and back down, using minimal pressure.

His breathing deepened, as did mine. I didn't want to stimulate him too much just yet, nor did I want to get caught looking at his alarm clock. I figured Sally wouldn't mind if my first gig—I refuse to call them tricks—went a little overtime, especially since she hadn't yet booked me with anyone else. After a while I reached into my purse, withdrew a condom, and placed it on the bed beside me. I sat up, knelt between his legs, and resumed touching him, now using both hands. He was beautifully aroused.

Just as I was about to reach for the condom, he opened his eyes, picked it up, opened the package, withdrew the slippery thing, and, smiling, handed it to me.

I rolled it slowly down his shaft, savoring his moan and his tightening muscles. Then I took him in my mouth for a few minutes. I knew he couldn't feel me too well through the condom—a girlfriend would never use one of those for a blow job—but it was the *idea* of what I was doing more than the actual doing of it. In appreciation, he throbbed a few times, sighed, and pushed up to me. Finally I withdrew, held his cock up, straddled him, and lowered myself slowly until his warm presence was completely inside me. I stayed a while, feeling him pulsate. I began rocking forward and back very slowly, his cool balls and strong thighs cushioning my butt. Then I raised myself almost to the tip and slowly sat back down. He felt good. I enjoyed doing all the work and assumed he knew it, but eventually he joined me with subtle motions. After a few minutes he throbbed powerfully, and I stopped. "Would you like to get on top?" I asked.

He smiled, raised himself on his elbows, lifted me as if I weighed nothing at all, got on his knees, turned, and gently set me down on my back, still fully inside me. He placed my ankles on his shoulders, supported himself on his hands, and began giving me the length of his cock, all the way in, all the way out, as slowly as we could stand it. That delicious torture didn't last long, and soon he was thrusting more aggressively. Suddenly I wondered how many of these appointments I could handle in one day, but this was a lovely debut. He was stimulating my clit and my G-spot with every stroke, and I started to come. He bent down and used his lips and tongue on my nipples, one after the other, until I exploded. Since the windows were open and I wanted to keep my voice down, we not only felt but also heard my *amrita*. He slowed down, released my legs, cupped his hands under my ass, and lowered himself to me. We lay still for a minute as my pulsations diminished. Finally he withdrew slowly, rose to his knees, and worked his way up until he was kneeling on either side of my breasts with that reddened cock close enough to kiss.

I guessed what he wanted, but I waited for his prompt.

He smiled, tugged on the empty tip of the condom,

and said, "If you would, please."

I reached up, pulled the condom off as patiently as possible, and set it on the edge of the bed.

There was a moment of silence as he trembled in front of me.

The sculptor reached to the nightstand, picked up a bottle of lube, and looked into my eyes.

When I smiled comprehendingly, he handed the bottle to me.

I poured a lot of it down his cock and a lot more of it into my left palm. I snapped the bottle shut, placed it back on the nightstand, and rubbed my hands together. As I brought them to bear on his taut manhood, I said softly, "Please try not to come in my hair, if you don't mind."

He smiled and held his hands aloft. "Where it goes is entirely up to you, dear."

Together we gathered most of my black hair under my head on the pillow and behind my neck and shoulders.

I'd been down this road before with boyfriends, but few things in life are as unpredictable as a guy's ejaculation. Given my own messy first climax downstairs, fair was fair. I knew what my artist wanted to see, but getting it to happen just so was another matter. I aimed his cock at my face and began stroking him more earnestly, above and below, with both hands. His excitement was thrilling, and scarcely less pronounced than my own. Soon he throbbed strongly, the pre-come spilling out like clear syrup. I knew this gun would kick when it shot and planned to compensate accordingly; still, the element of chance prevailed.

Eventually he was thrusting powerfully, his abdomen

contracting, thighs tense. I felt his balls draw up and the shaft harden even more, and he moaned deeply. Finally his whole body vibrated. "Oh, God!" he said loudly. Then he came.

My, *my,* did he come! It seemed like a dozen hot thick white spurts went everywhere. I managed to get most of it to splash in my face, but inevitably some did reach the top of my head; and the large amount streaming down my temples and cheeks would soon reach the hair we'd so carefully tucked out of the way. I'd tried to keep my eyes open throughout—I knew he'd like that—but it wasn't easy.

I'm used to men breaking out in the laughter of release after an ejaculation—I love that word, *ejaculation*—and my sculptor was definitely enjoying himself. I kept stroking him lightly till his throbs subsided, then wrapped my hands warmly around him. He was positively burning with sexual energy.

"When you have a moment," he grinned breathlessly, "check out the headboard."

I looked up to see that a huge spurt, presumably his first, had flown there and was running down the teak wood toward my now hopeless coif. Silently I agreed that the afternoon had been worth a second shampoo.

After his orgasm had thoroughly resolved—though the amazing erection showed no signs of relaxing—he eased down beside me, took a towel from the nightstand, and began what little damage control he could offer. "I wish I could photograph you this way," he smiled.

I figured that was as good a cue as any. "You don't recognize me, do you?"

He pulled back and fixed me with those Paul Newman

eyes. "You know, I've been thinking you do look familiar."

I said nothing as he resumed dabbing at my skin.

"I attend so many local events and belong to so many local organizations," he continued, "and it's impossible to live in this town without running into someone you know every day."

Men crack me up. I decided just to let it go. If eventually he remembered our connection, I trusted him to keep this day to himself.

After he'd cleaned me up to the extent possible, he replaced the towel and resumed stroking my hair as tenderly as a doting husband. "Where are you from?" he asked.

I was glad he hadn't asked me my real name, which I'm afraid I'd have told him in a second. "New York City."

"Yeah?" he replied. "So am I."

We then shared brief bios, concluding that we probably knew some of the same people. He still hadn't figured out how we knew each other here, but I didn't care—especially when he said he'd love to see me again.

At the door, I finally got to see him soft: just as beautiful. It was like saying goodbye to a Florentine statue that had sprung to life just for me. The televised come shots were still sailing in the background.

Unfortunately, the next time we met was two hours after I'd been with another client—who happened to have the biggest, ugliest cock I'd ever seen. This thing was eight and a half inches long, as its owner only too proudly informed me, and correspondingly fat. It was bigger soft than many guys are erect. When it finally got hard, which seemed to take forever, it bent the wrong way in two directions: down and to the right (his left). The skin was splotchy and riddled with blue veins. *Ugh.* To top it off, he wasn't circumcised. OK, I'm sorry, I know that practice is outdated and unnecessary, and probably traumatic to the subconscious—little wonder men are so screwed up about their equipment—but I just think an uncut cock is gross. I knew on day one that I'd have to get over that to continue in this business, but it's much easier to fake affection for a beautiful cock than one that looks like it belongs on a farm animal. Anyway, I was not looking forward to facing my handsome artist two hours after experiencing this other dude's disgusting, uncomfortable schlong.

Not surprisingly, my sculptor—please forgive my consistent omission of his name, since I'm pretty sure you know him—picked up on my disappointment as soon as he entered me and saw the pain on my face. He withdrew gently, went down and kissed me there several times, and lay at my side. We talked for a while and went downstairs, still naked. He cooked me a delightful light supper, and then we went out on the deck, smoked a bowl, and spent about twenty minutes in his hot tub. By then it was full dark. He turned on the exterior lights and showed me around the other humorously erotic sculptures that peopled his estate. We had to move fast to outrun the mosquitoes; but it was exciting to explore this guy's private world naked, knowing his neighbors either couldn't see us through the dense foliage or possibly wouldn't complain if they could. We finished the evening on the sofa, sans pornography, with what he assured me was the greatest hand job he'd ever received. This time he came in his own hair and face, to our mutual delight.

The sculpture gardener remains my favorite client. We see each other about once a month. I kind of wish we'd met and become intimate before I'd put my professional reputation on hold, but I've been around long enough to know that familiarity breeds contempt. I definitely can handle twelve times a year.

Could you turn that off now, please? Well, look at *you!*

SECOND THOUGHTS

Jamie Gales, twenty-three, lay on the lower bunk with her head resting in her new cellmate's lap. Twenty-nine-year-old Tabitha Goodwin listened to Jamie's story, dabbed at the girl's tears with a black cotton bandanna, and stayed alert for the guard's footsteps: intimacy of any kind was strictly forbidden.

"I wasn't thinking about where we were," Jamie said, repeating what she had told the judge. "I just pushed."

Jamie recently had begun serving thirty years for second-degree murder. In exchange for a guilty plea, authorities had dropped the capital charge of first-degree murder, which requires premeditation. Jamie had surprised the court by confessing that she had shoved her husband off the South Rim of the Grand Canyon on the second day of their honeymoon.

Suddenly Jamie giggled and gently moved Tabitha's hand away. "I can't believe I just remembered this," she whispered, realigning herself on the thin mattress, "but when I was twelve my family visited the Canyon. We were walking along the path, which isn't all that far from the edge, when we came upon this young couple standing on the canyon side of the guardrail. The girl was taking the guy's picture as he stood facing her with that incredible scene in the background—I mean, no photograph does it justice. She kept telling him to step back as she focused the camera, and when we passed them we joked among ourselves that maybe she was trying to bump him off. Apparently that wasn't it, because we saw them later in the lodge."

Jamie's trouble had begun in early childhood, when her parents' cruel, vindictive arguments would send the only child hiding in her bedroom with her head buried in pillows. In high school, Jamie wrote a social-studies term paper stating that marriage was an illogical, outdated, destructive institution: few other animals practiced monogamy, the observance of marriage began when human life expectancy was less than half what it is today, the religions that embraced the notion of marriage were nullified by hypocrisy, the species stood a better chance of survival if healthy men could scatter their seed without condemnation, and the sheer boredom of waking next to the same person every morning for decades was inconceivable. Jamie's middle-aged male teacher gave her an A and advised her to major in psychology.

Jamie eschewed college and remained a loner. She surrendered occasionally to brief relationships with guys and to a month-long fling with another girl, but she lost interest at the first sign of possessive behavior. Rarely would Jamie spend the night with a lover, and when she did insomnia would force her to slip out before sunrise. She babysat neighbors' kids during the day and worked odd jobs at night to avoid needing a roommate to share her expenses.

No one was more surprised than Jamie herself when at twenty-one she accepted the marriage proposal of Cory Jackman, a twenty-seven-year-old commercial airline pilot. Cory had won Jamie with assurances that his frequent absences would keep their flame alive, that he had grown up in a similarly dysfunctional family and understood Jamie's reluctance, and that their union would serve mainly as domestic security for two admitted misfits. The couple's guest list comprised only a few friends and did not include their parents.

Jamie had borrowed her wedding dress from a daycare client, Sally Bierce, who testified at Jamie's trial that the reliable girl found it difficult to interact with other adults but that her two children loved Jamie. Erin Siegel, a harpsichordist Jamie had commissioned to write a piece for the couple's first dance, testified that Jamie was quiet and aloof but seemed happily reconciled to her future. Jamie's defense team showed the jurors photographs and videos of Jamie smiling as she had her hair done and tried on her borrowed dress. Prosecutors argued that Jamie was cold and dispassionate, had made it known that she abhorred marriage, and in her disappointment had lured her faithful provider to a dangerous precipice and deliberately pushed him to his death.

On that day, Jamie and Cory had strolled a long distance on the canyon rim. They stopped for a picnic lunch behind some trees that lined the cliff and shielded the couple from other tourists. Jamie had noticed Cory watching another young woman as she walked ahead of them along the path, and the new bride had registered the return of Cory's undivided attention after the woman met up with friends and headed toward a parking lot. Jamie brought up the subject while the couple folded their blanket. She said she did not feel the way she thought a newlywed should feel. Cory reddened and loudly denied his wife's accusation, dropping his half of the blanket and stepping toward her. He grabbed her left wrist painfully and warned her that this line of thinking would destroy what promised to be an agreeable long-distance relationship. Jamie snatched back her arm and used her other hand to push Cory away. She watched incredulously as her husband tripped on a root and fell backward over the edge. Jamie would never forget his chilling high-pitched scream and the sickening crack as Cory's body slammed into a stone outcropping and sailed, broken and silent, to the mile-deep canyon floor.

In shock, Jamie failed to call for help or to report Cory's disappearance until the next day. When she did, she told authorities that her husband had spent the previous night at a local bar and had not returned.

Cellmate Tabitha Goodwin twirled her left fingertips through Jamie's soft blonde hair and slipped her right hand under Jamie's T-shirt. "You safe now, baby," she whispered. "Them motherfuckers can't do shit to you long as I'm around, and I ain't goin' nowhere."

THE SIREN OF SALT LAKE CITY

Lynne, whose last name is none of *my* business, let alone the reader's, seduced me into the most foolish one-nighter of my life. I met her on the road; she was a hotel busgirl. I was thirty-seven. Lynne was sixteen. Madness.

Our group was performing in a large circular ballroom with the stage located in the middle. A low latticework fence enclosed the platform, but anyone who felt like it could reach over and touch the musicians or their instruments. That was just one of the reasons we hated the place.

I caught this girl eyeing me during a set, smiled back, and returned my thoughts to the music. When next my eyes drifted in her direction, though, she was still there, smiling invitingly. She looked young, of course, but not that young. She had long brown hair, a cute perky face, and a tight petite figure. But still. I tried to avoid her eyes. Toward the end of the set, having noticed her immovable attention a few more times, I looked up once more to see she had gone. There was a small folded piece of paper atop my amplifier.

Lynne did not wait for me to go to my room and dial her number, which I would not have done. She accosted me during a break and made it plain she would be awaiting me at the end of the night. I tried to be both friendly and remote, to no avail.

When the gig was over, as I gathered my things, there she was, positioned discreetly in a corner, visible only to me. There was no reason for this to be a setup, either on her part or as a prank launched by my bandmates. I figured it could do no harm to take her aside and talk some sense into her pretty little head.

After confirming that everyone else had disappeared for the night, I made my way over to Lynne. I gave her a look I hoped she would interpret as, *This is crazy; go home,* but apparently it said, *Yes, you're the cutest thing I've seen in months, and I'd love to fuck you right here and now.* Lynne took my hand and led me outside to a dark corner of the building. She looked more worldly in the moonlight. She eased me back against the wall, looked into my eyes, and kissed me. It was the hard, desperate kiss of a rural teenager. I pulled back and took the trembling girl in my arms.

"We can't do this," I whispered. "Do you know how old I am?" She smelled sweet.

"I don't care," she said.

What did she see in me? I was going to disappear in twelve hours. Maybe that was the idea.

"We could get in a lot of trouble," I continued, convinced I was telling her nothing new.

Lynne reached up and kissed me again, more patiently this time. She pressed her taut body against me. Her neck was baby-soft. We kissed again, stroking each other's back. She was as firm as an Olympic diver. Suddenly she reached down and cupped her tiny palm over the bulge in my pants.

I started a little and smiled. Someday she would see the humor in it too, but for now she was on a mission. Lynne caressed my warm cock. My mind raced, summarizing a limited grasp of the judicial system. *Doesn't this state still use the firing squad?* Lynne's heartbreaking brown eyes sparkled in the warm night air. I kissed her and gently ran my fingers over her perfect little ass. She closed her hand around my cock and moaned.

OK, no intercourse, I resolved as we walked in the shadows toward my van. She was quiet, clinging warmly to me as I nestled her in my shoulder. We got inside and drove without lights to a distant corner of the parking lot. I kept the motor running.

In moments Lynne and I were spread out on blankets, kissing and running feverish hands over each other. She unsnapped her bra, and no sooner had I glided my palm over her pure mounds than she was working on my zipper. Lynne slipped her little hand in and wrapped it artlessly around my cock. She was precious.

I wanted to please her, but Lynne had the good sense to lower her jeans just enough to reveal the beautiful curves of her hips.

Her tiny vagina was delightful, and she shivered with excitement. "I wish I could have you inside me," she whispered.

I admired her for having set a limit and felt relieved enough to enjoy our brief misdemeanor.

Lynne twitched under my fingerwork for some time. I do not think she had an orgasm, if indeed she had ever had one. Finally, Lynne looked knowingly at me and relaxed. I kissed her and, with some reluctance, withdrew my hand from her wet panties. I held her tightly and spanked her softly a few times. We laughed. Not at the same things, probably.

Lynne uncurled her fingers from my cock and brought her hand up, but not out. She tugged at the waistband. With renewed determination she squirmed to free her other hand as she continued trying to yank down my pants. I was almost too charmed to help her, but eventually I raised myself and turned up on my back. Lynne smiled at my hard, weeping organ. Without so much as a moment's lightness she got up on her knees and began masturbating me. Not too well. I tried to remember anyone who during my teens had worked me successfully with motions like these, but I could not. I did not want to insult her, but I knew the girl was not going to get anywhere this way. After a few minutes I pulled her gently down to my side.

"Relax your hand."

She smiled curiously.

I wrapped my hand carefully around hers. "Just stay."

She intuitively tightened her grasp a little.

Slowly I began moving her hand, pacing the strokes, and Lynne understood. Her breathing raced. I removed my hand, and Lynne took over.

As my own excitement grew, Lynne began to shift her position. I worried that my pupil was becoming distracted; but with her free hand she was unbuttoning her blouse. She moved her own hips as the light cotton fell away from her little pink nipples. I drew her face to me and kissed her. She pointed my cock toward her chest.

"Yes," I whispered. She shook as if inside me, soft cries

escaping as she covered my face and neck with kisses. When the orgasm subsided, she kept her hand on me. Slowly we relaxed.

A long pause.

"Um, have you ever done that before?" she asked in her childlike voice.

"Not like that," I assured her.

"Thanks. I liked it."

"I did too."

I reached over and massaged Lynne's glistening skin, smiling as her eyes drifted shut. "Will you be uncomfortable going home like this?" I asked.

"I want it there," she replied softly.

We embraced quietly. Finally we rearranged ourselves, said a melancholy farewell, and drove back to the front of the hotel. We agreed to go in separately, Lynne first, since her ride—her mother, that is—probably was wondering why she had not called.

It seemed we had pulled this one off. I walked to our group's suite amazed, relieved, and ashamed, looking occasionally over my shoulder.

I entered to the sound of muffled snickering. My bandmates had observed Lynne's courtship in the club and until now had refrained from mentioning it. Back on team turf, I was fair game.

"You didn't fuck her, did you?" Brad, the bandleader, asked from his bed.

"Of course not," I replied, unnecessarily admitting where I had been. A long silence ensued, indicating the committee expected a full report. "It was strictly manual labor," I humored them. The poor bastards laughed enviously, though they got their turns often enough in our travels. "Now, let's try to keep it down in here," I smiled, easing into the crisp white sheets.

The next morning, we went downstairs, packed up our gear, and sat down to breakfast. The guys kept their ribbing to a minimum. Toward the end of the meal, Brad rose to collect our paycheck from the office.

When he returned, his face was ashen. He sat down close and fixed me in a judgmental glare. "What did you say that girl's name was?" he demanded.

I had not mentioned the girl's name, but that was beside the point. "Lynne," I whispered.

"Well," Brad continued sternly, "we're about to go out to the lobby and meet her parents."

My heart leapt to my throat. I calculated the shortest route through the back window and around to my van before the lynch mob spotted me. What had happened? Had Lynne been reckless enough to tell someone? Had her mom picked up our scent? Had not Lynne said her dad was a *cop,* for Christ's sake? My career, my whole stupid life was over.

Brad let me hang in this agony for several long seconds before surrendering to a broad smile.

"You asshole," I said, heaving a chestful of deliverance.

It was the most instructive feeling I had experienced since the night in college when I fell asleep at the wheel on a mountain road and woke just in time. For years thereafter I searched high and low for an opportunity to get Brad back for his masterpiece. I never did.

SYBIL AND BIFF

Nearly topping the criteria for my choice of a college to attend was the permission to own a car on campus during my freshman year. I actually turned down a couple of superior schools because they wisely forbade this reckless distraction. At one of those better institutions I might have learned more about things that matter and less about things that do not, from which it follows that I would have had considerably less fun. But my rationale for requiring a car was merely practical: I expected to play off-campus gigs in addition to my curricular activities and needed a vehicle for my gear.

It turned out that the campus parking permit for my 1967 Volkswagen Bus cost more than I needed to pay: immediately on arriving I learned I could park for free on the safe streets of Doctors' Hill, an affluent section of town just outside the bucolic campus. Whenever I had a gig I would walk the quarter mile from my dorm to my Bus in my hippie stage clothes, ignoring bemused glances from my conservative classmates. I kept several of my dad's old army blankets in the back of the Bus, both for covering my unattended equipment and for softening the floor on those occasions when guitars and amplifiers could make room for a girl. The neighborhood was so benign that in temperate weather I could leave my gear overnight in the Bus, something I would never do today. Among the items that spent most of their time in my vehicle was one of those vinyl-upholstered Kustom amps that looked like something out of a cheap diner.

My sophomore-year roommate was a drama major named Bill Ruud. On the night he opened in *The Lion in Winter,* I was otherwise engaged in the music building. I had seen the film, with Katharine Hepburn and Peter O'Toole, not exactly a fair comparison. Bill and I had grinned at the coincidence that his real-life girlfriend was named Eleanor, as in *Aquitaine.* Finishing my work in time to catch the last forty-five minutes, I slipped into the theater and stood in the dark doorway. After a while I became aware of an alluring presence beside me.

She was pretty, with milky skin, imploring dark eyes, full lips, and long, shiny brown hair. I had never seen her on campus. She was standing much closer to me than necessary. By the end of the play we were touching lightly, whispering occasionally, her fragrance drawing me in as she smiled with undue familiarity.

Bill had invited me to the cast party, and I had expected to pass. Suddenly it seemed as though I might have a date.

As the lights came up, she said, "Sounds like fun."

We were halfway to the party before we introduced ourselves. We arrived, endured our share of the affected conversation of young actors, and slipped quietly into the night. Within the hour we were parked in an abandoned construction site, the autumn breeze passing through open windows to dry the sweat of our exertion.

Sybil and I learned very little about each other. I do not remember her major, if I ever knew it. She was a local country girl—her surname was well established throughout the region—whose only domestic gesture was to feed me once at her mother's, after which she straddled me on the living-room sofa while her mom sat on her bed watching an old detective movie with the door closed. Sybil and I got together several times that fall.

We took an overnight trip together; in a rural motel room, with massive oak trees rustling outside, we did it literally all night long. We did it in my pre-coed dorm room. We did it in nature. We even did it late one night in the basement of her church. We never fell in love, but Sybil and I were seriously in bed.

Bill Ruud's girlfriend, Eleanor, got pregnant toward the end of the second semester, and I emptied my bank account over the weekend so they could arrange for a safe and, in those days, illegal abortion. As promised, they repaid me the following week; as a bonus, they invited me to a little Sunday-afternoon picnic in a park at the bottom of Doctors' Hill.

At that event I met their friend Biff, a petite, erudite English major with long, straight auburn hair announced by a wall of bangs. She had big brown eyes, a thin turned-up nose, slight but sensuous lips, and a sweet girlish voice that was quick to blossom in bright laughter. We were spread out on the grass in the welcoming April sunshine finishing a bottle of cheap red wine by the time I asked the inevitable question of her unusual first name, which turned out to have been the result of her little brother's inability to pronounce the word *Elizabeth*—lucky for me, since that was my mother's name, and who wants *that* image in his head? Biff and I lay there kissing tenderly, almost platonically, me on my back, she above me at a severe angle, our hands kept chastely to ourselves, restrained by shyness and by Bill and Eleanor's giggling presence on the adjacent blanket. As the sun began brushing the treetops, Eleanor suggested I drive us up to Reddish Knob, the highest peak in a cluster of nearby Blue Ridge undulations. Out of respect for my new acquaintance, I withheld comment on the landmark's suggestive name.

The drive took nearly an hour—mountains always look closer than they are—and we spent only a few minutes at the summit, shivering in the cool wind that accompanied a stunning twilight panorama. On the way up, Biff had sat in the passenger seat, reaching over now and then to massage my hand, smiling discreetly in silence as Bill and Eleanor made out on the backseat. Before returning to the campus, the four of us shared a joint in the Bus. As we descended the mountain, Biff and I could hear the sounds of belt buckles and breathless invitations behind us. Biff moved closer to me, perching atop my padded Kustom speaker cabinet. She brushed my forearm as I ran my fingertips lightly up and down her thighs. Biff did not object when I began applying gossamer strokes between her legs, nor did she make any audible sounds, unbutton her jeans, reach for me, or otherwise encourage her fascinated companion. When I dropped Biff off at her dorm, she kissed me lightly on the lips and went inside. In a moment the scent of her hair had given way to that of boxwood and the sounds of crickets.

Biff and I shared lunch together in the campus dining hall the following week, quite by accident; we happened to have been standing in line together. We talked politely, she told me of the busy summer she expected back home, and that was it. I have no idea where she is today, how many people still call her Biff, or how I might find out; I never learned her last name.

Several years after graduation I read in the alumni magazine that Bill Ruud, who had traded the theater of drama for that of surgery, died of pancreatic cancer. Last I heard, his old flame Eleanor, who remained single and childless, was running a small branch of Planned Parenthood in South Carolina.

THE TEFLON
HAYSEED

Garth Vance was a short, fat, illiterate bumpkin from Gilbert, Arkansas, population thirty-three. In the face, he resembled a cross between Jackie Gleason and Queen Victoria. He stuffed much of his long, shapeless beige hair under one of several baseball caps advertising working-class recreational products. He lived his life in slow motion.

Garth liked to fish. He did not much enjoy or understand any other entertainment, particularly if it involved mental or physical effort. His wit began and ended with the claim that he had majored in English, an absurdity that withered under fifteen seconds of conversation. Garth had eked out an associate's degree from Ouachita Technical College in Malvern, but no evidence existed of whatever he had learned there. On his fortieth birthday, with nothing to keep him in Arkansas but a history of menial jobs and a nagging mother, Garth moved to Stock Island, Florida, a depressed fishing village whose populace did the dirty work of neighboring Key West. Garth found immediate employment washing boats, worked his way up to mate on a charter vessel, and set his sights on the captain's license that one day would allow him to ferry rich tourists around the Lower Keys. Garth lived for a few months in a trailer with a short, fat, illiterate hairdresser he had met at the Hogfish Bar and Grill, but she soon reclaimed her self-respect and kicked him out. With what remained of his savings, Garth bought a small boat moored at the Safe Harbour Marina and moved aboard. Garth struggled to make a living among established commercial fishermen and kept his eye out for a steady job that he would not actually have to perform.

One day Garth saw a help-wanted ad in the *Key West Citizen* seeking a part-time van driver for the Monroe County Public Library. Since the library system's five branches were spread over the hundred-mile length of the Keys, the cataloging department, which was attached to the Key West branch, maintained a weekly "book run" to deliver new materials and retrieve interlibrary loans—this despite the fact that county taxpayers already financed a courier service for this sort of activity. A normal person, raised in the civilized world and having acquired its work ethic, could perform the book run in five or six hours. Sitting in his boat sipping *café con leche* with the newspaper spread over his elephantine lap while ignoring the stench of gasoline, sewage, polluted water, rotting seaweed, and decaying fish heads, Garth figured correctly that he could stretch this simple drive up and down U.S. 1 into an all-day affair. Thus he could minimize the amount of time he would need to spend cataloging library materials, an occupation requiring intelligence, cultural literacy, a working knowledge of foreign languages, the ability to adapt to new procedures and technologies, attention to detail, punctuality, and other qualities that Garth lacked.

Fit, affable Jim Baines, sixty, had headed the library

cataloging department for twenty-four years and regarded the next three hundred sixty-five days as the threshold to retirement and a new life. The career librarian and amateur actor from Rockville, Maryland, had come to Key West to explore its lively theater scene and, more specifically, its colorful gay community. Jim had long before accepted the Keys' low professional standards in all fields and rarely expected a job applicant to present a less than laughable résumé. Having begun his career during the days of the wooden card catalog and the minimal bibliographic information that format entailed, Jim had transitioned to the current computerized systems with ease but without a full grasp of the digital world's far more stringent technical requirements. He therefore weighed Garth Vance's ridiculous credentials against the wishful thinking that Garth could do little damage to the library catalog during the mere twenty hours a week the fool would spend at his desk. Having been advised to avoid undue stress and excitement because of hereditary heart disease, Jim turned Garth's training over to fiftyish Earline Sanders, the short, fat, illiterate cataloger Jim reluctantly had promoted to his second in command. Jim was sorry he had ever met Garth and Earline by the time Garth completed his required six-month probationary period, after which to get fired a county employee practically would have to shoot the president of the United States on national television.

Garth showed up for work dressed for the beach, in flip-flops, a bathing suit, and a tie-dyed T-shirt that barely covered his massive gut; this would remain his daily attire, uncorrected by management. Garth spent most of his in-house time perusing Facebook and other inappropriate Web sites, checking his personal e-mail, taking personal phone calls, sleeping, sneaking outdoors for smoke breaks, or waddling around the building to socialize with well-paid staffers who on any given day could be observed standing around with nothing to do. Jim Baines would opine that Garth's taking forever to perform the book run was his one welcome deficiency, since it got Garth's worthless ass out of the building for one whole day a week.

The cataloging position vacated by Earline's promotion remained open, and neither Garth nor Earline could tackle the mountain of unprocessed materials that had accumulated at a fourth desk. By the time Jim hired fit fellow Washingtonian Horst Heimlich, a desperate fifty-three-year-old novelist and musician who was everything Garth and Earline would never be, the backlog of books, audiobooks, compact discs, digital videodiscs, and other materials had attained Himalayan proportions. Horst surmounted this summit well before his own probationary period lapsed, by which time he was reeling with disbelief at the county government's well-documented culture of incompetence. Garth's words of welcome to Horst had been, "Hey, man, it's the county: you don't have to work to get paid."

The Bubba System eventually saw fit to promote Garth Vance to full-time status, thus granting him two more days a week in which to defile the catalog with egregious errors. Horst Heimlich's protests on behalf of the international scholars, writers, and students who used the catalog online or on the premises to research Ernest Hemingway, Tennessee Williams, Henry Flagler, and other figures important to Keys history fell on deaf ears.

Equally appalling to Horst was Garth Vance's behavior, blessed by his supervisor, Earline Sanders: redneck music blasted through leaky earbuds, continual uninformed small talk, obscene language, and disgusting personal habits that included loud yawning, burping, farting, hawking and spitting into his wastebasket, and lengthy coughing fits brought on by a lifetime of chain smoking. By midday the cataloging department smelled and sounded like the Schooner Wharf Bar. Since both Garth and Earline were hideously obese, they maintained a freezing room temperature that forced Jim and Horst to wear sweaters and use space heaters throughout the year. Every day Garth asked Earline how to perform some task he should have learned in his first week; every day Horst had to listen to both of them spin their wheels over things they should have learned in high school.

Those county librarians who were not confined to these close quarters found Garth's rusticated ways to be quite entertaining. No one thought him more charming than library-system director Nadine Kaiser, whose refusal to support her few qualified employees was matched only by her lack of vision and leadership. Nadine's advice to Horst was to "lighten up."

Jim Baines shared Horst's abhorrence for the situation but, to protect his fragile health and to stay focused on his imminent escape, offered no more help than Nadine. Eventually Horst was compelled to go over everyone's head, which only deepened his resentment for the byzantine county bureaucracy.

At the end of the workday one afternoon after pleading

yet again with Earline to curb Garth's uncouth habits, Horst exited the building and walked toward his car. Garth, having overheard Horst's appeal, confronted him in the parking lot and shouted the slogan of his tribe: "Fuck you!" The next day, the musical author nearly missed a book-signing event because of two symmetrically placed nails he discovered in one of his car tires. Finally, after Horst invited his attorney, the county administrator, the county commissioners, and the county sheriff into the conversation, the office atmosphere improved by about one percent.

Late one evening a few months later, after his customary series of nightcaps at the local Moose lodge, and on the heels of two traffic accidents in the library van and several reckless-driving citations in his own pickup truck, Garth Vance was arrested for driving while under the influence of alcohol. He hired a local lawyer who specialized in such cases—a thriving business in boozy Monroe County. Garth paid an additional two thousand dollars to suppress a prior DUI conviction in Arkansas, thus enabling him to plead no contest to a first offense. After months of routine delays, Garth was tried and convicted. His driver's license could have been suspended for five years, but the judge reduced that period to six months. The library system did not discipline Garth in any way. During the months of Garth's suspension, Horst and other legitimate personnel were forced to perform the book run, hoping that no one they knew outside their day job saw them doing so. The Key West branch invented other undignified charades to justify Garth's presence: he was stationed at the overstaffed circulation desk, where his sloppy appearance and literary ignorance did little to improve the Keys' "laid-back" image (more than one patron mistook Garth for one of the vagrants who frequented the building to soak up air-conditioning and to watch porn on the public computers); Garth was put in charge of recycling, even though county taxpayers already employed a company for this purpose; Garth was appointed "safety officer" and entrusted with orchestrating fire drills, raising and lowering Old Glory, and other rituals, even though the Key West branch recently had hired several young employees who could easily have handled these sidelines; and Garth became the designated beast of burden whenever someone decided to relocate a piece of furniture, even though manual labor was the domain of the county public-works department.

Today Garth Vance is back behind the wheel and performing his delightful antics for his loyal fans. He looks forward to his annual five-percent raise. The Monroe County Board of County Commissioners is proud to employ such a person to help escort its endangered libraries into the paperless future.

THE TIME TRAVELER OF NAPLES

A second nonfiction interlude, based on the fact that truth is often stranger than fiction

Italian composer Carlo Gesualdo (1566-1613), Prince of Venosa, was sort of the Hieronymus Bosch of music. Gesualdo was born fifty years after Bosch's death, but the nobleman's eccentric and ethereally beautiful harmony, centuries ahead of its time, brings to mind, among other things, the Dutch painter's disturbing, fantastical imagery. A musicologist might scoff at that comparison, but the lay reader is more likely to have seen a print of *The Garden of Earthly Delights* than to have heard of Carlo Gesualdo. (Supporting evidence is that Bosch's name appears in the biographical appendix of *Merriam-Webster's Collegiate Dictionary* but that Gesualdo's does not.) Another way to describe the sound of Gesualdo's music might be to imagine a neurotic Claude Debussy magically transported back to the sixteenth century.

Gesualdo's radical chromaticism had its roots in the much milder innovations of Renaissance composers working in the northern Italian city of Ferrara, which the Neapolitan prince would revisit to marry his second wife. But no one before 1900 ever wrote such consistently daring music: reason enough to know this fascinating musician's work. Gesualdo was also a virtuoso lutenist, though little evidence exists of his writing lute music or accompanied song. His oeuvre consists mainly of five-part *a cappella* choral music, partly because flexible human voices could negotiate strange intervals more pleasantly than the *meantone-tempered* (rigidly tuned) instruments of Gesualdo's day.

The main reason your average music major remembers the Prince of Venosa is that he murdered his first wife and her lover *in flagrante delicto*. The Coen brothers could do worse than to give tunesmith Carter Burwell the year off and base their next Hollywood blockbuster on the life of Carlo Gesualdo. (Filmmaker Werner Herzog did direct a documentary on the prince in 1995; see bibliography.)

Carlo was born on March 30, 1566, to an aristocratic family with deep ties to King Philip II of Spain and to Pope Pius IV. (Carlo's birthdate was disputed until as recently as 1985.) Carlo spent much of his infancy in Taurasi, a town not far from the picturesque medieval village that bears his family name. In 1740 the village of Gesualdo would prove to have been the site of Paestum, the oldest Greek colony in Italy. Carlo's mother died when he was seven, and his uncle Carlo, for whom the child was named, sent him to Rome to pursue an ecclesiastical career. Carlo was placed under the protection of another uncle, Alfonso, dean of the College of Cardinals. But with the premature death of his older brother, Luigi, in 1584, and his father's passing in 1591, Carlo, now the eighth Count of Conza and the third Prince of Venosa, was forced to become head of one of the wealthiest estates in southern Italy.

Given Carlo's lineage, his marriage had been promptly

arranged. In 1586, Carlo, only twenty, took as his wife Maria D'Avalos, a cousin who was descended from Spanish royalty, four years Carlo's senior, and already twice widowed. Maria was famous for her beauty and charm, and tales of extramarital affairs soon became public. Yet another of Carlo's uncles, Giulio, turned out to have been one of Maria's unsuccessful suitors and assured the humiliated nephew of his wife's unfaithfulness.

Women were not permitted the amorous dalliances that men enjoyed in Renaissance Italy, a double standard that persists throughout the world today. Late in life Carlo Gesualdo would admit having fathered an illegitimate child of his own, but he escaped retaliation because he outranked his mistress. According to tradition in Spanish-influenced Naples, a cuckolded male, particularly a Neapolitan prince, had not only the right but also the duty to protect his family name by killing the adulterous couple. (Custom in northern Italy called for dispatching only the blushing bride.)

One day Carlo announced he was going hunting, thus laying the trap for Maria and the Duke of Andria. The two met in Carlo's residence, the Palazzo San Severo, across the street from San Domenico, the church where Carlo and Maria had been married. Carlo and a party of servants entered the love nest and murdered Maria and the duke in their bed. Details of the gruesome act circulated quickly and included firsthand reports of gory nightshirts, slit throats, mutilated genitalia, and Carlo's immediate return to the scene, knife in bloody hand, to ensure that his wife was dead.

In typical Catholic fashion, Carlo Gesualdo bounced

back from infamy relatively unscathed. In February 1594, he married Eleonora d'Este (also older than he), whose estate at Ferrara would otherwise have reverted to the papacy because the reigning duke, Alfonso II, was childless. Since Gesualdo's connection to Ferrara had been through its progressive musical life, he thoughtfully brought along his first two books of madrigals and two of his court musicians. The lavish wedding ceremonies lasted several days. The suit of armor Duke Alfonso II gave Carlo can be seen today in the museum of Konopiste Castle near Prague.

Carlo's noble marital prospects had canceled out his uxoricidal past, but word soon circulated that the prince was subjecting his new wife to physical and psychological abuse. He cheated on her, traveled widely without her, focused his attention on music and magic, and turned eventually to his only true friend, Jesus Christ.

Today Carlo Gesualdo would be diagnosed as *bipolar,* a threadbare term that hardly describes the composer's personal problems and idiosyncrasies. He indulged in self-flagellation and maintained a team of young men to beat him into states of ecstasy; the latter masochism fulfilled the alternate purpose of helping to relieve the prince's chronic constipation. His confused sexual orientation was just one of many insecurities. He became involved in the witch trials of two women who, under torture by the Inquisition, confessed to giving the prince poisonous love potions and purgatives containing menstrual blood and Carlo's own semen. To counteract the effects of these treatments and to battle his asthma, Carlo ingested a traditional aristocratic "unicorn powder" made from the horns of cows. In addition to his religious piety, Carlo practiced the other superstitions of his time, including astrology, numerology, and symbology. The shocking twists and turns of the composer's harmonic progressions expressed the severe melancholia that sorcerers, exorcists, and charlatans could not cure. His paranoia surfaced in accusations that musical rivals had plagiarized his work: no mean feat, considering Gesualdo's unique musical palette. And like George Harrison, the metaphysically inclined "quiet Beatle" of the twentieth century, Carlo Gesualdo could talk your ear off.

Gesualdo's reputation as a composer rests mostly on his highly chromatic secular madrigals, filled with sexual symbolism, and on the somewhat more conservative *Responsoria* for Holy Week. The former works were examples of *musica reservata* or *musica segreta,* music intended for the private use of the composer and his inner circle; some pieces may have been meant for Carlo's ears alone. Carlo signed these works not with his name but with his family crest, designating them as personal property. Gesualdo published the *Responsoria* late in life not only to cement his musical legacy but also as part of a broad appeal for redemption that included the commissioning of a richly symbolized altarpiece for his church, Santa Maria delle Grazie, the establishment of a Capuchin monastery on his estate, and the building of the Chapel of St. Ignatius Loyola (who would not be canonized until 1622) in the Neapolitan Jesuit church of Gesù Nuovo.

The location of Gesualdo's final resting place is uncertain because a devastating earthquake in 1688 destroyed the composer's intended gravesite beneath the

Naples chapel altar. Gesualdo's daughter-in-law verified that the composer's body was placed initially in a side chapel in Santa Maria delle Grazie in Gesualdo until the completion of the Loyola chapel. The powerful marble statues of Jeremiah and David by Cosimo Fanzago that flank the chapel altar may therefore preside over an empty grave.

As an abstract listening experience, Gesualdo's art, like that of a more famously anguished composer, Beethoven, is completely at odds with the grim story of his life—only the thinnest surface of which is addressed here. It is sublime music, and no better proof exists that in every human being there is good.

BIBLIOGRAPHY

Gesualdo, Carlo. *Madrigaux*. Les Arts Florissants, William Christie, conductor. Lyon: Harmonia Mundi (France) HMG501268, 1992. Compact discs.

_____. *Responsoria, Sacrae Cantiones*. Centro Musica Antica di Padova, Livio Picotti, conductor. London: Argo/Decca 430832-2, 1991. Compact disc.

_____. *Tenebrae*. Hilliard Ensemble. München: ECM 78118-21422-2, 1991. Compact discs.

_____. *Tenebrae Responsories for Holy Saturday*. Tallis Scholars, Peter Phillips, conductor. Oxford: Gimel CDGIM 015, 2002. Compact disc.

Gesualdo: Death for Five Voices: A Film by Werner Herzog. Halle/Saale: Arthaus-Musik 102055, 1995. Videodisc.

Watkins, Glenn. *The Gesualdo Hex: Music, Myth, and Memory*. New York: Norton, 2010.

_____. *Gesualdo: The Man and His Music,* 2nd ed. Oxford: Oxford, 1991.

THE TRINITY
OF REGRET

Non, je ne regrette rien. "No regrets." *Bullshit.*

It was not singer Edith Piaf's delusions that occupied the old man's thoughts with increasing frequency but rather those of actor Jason Robards, who, playing a dying television producer in Paul Thomas Anderson's 1999 film *Magnolia,* tells a nurse from his deathbed, "This is the regret that you make. The goddamned regret! I let my love go. Don't let *anyone* ever say to you you shouldn't regret anything. You regret what you fuckin' want. *Use* that regret. A little moral. Love, love, *love.* Life ain't short; it's long. It's *long,* goddamn it. Oh! What did I do?"

And the old man did use his regret.

As an agnostic former Catholic, the old man liked grouping things in threes. This fetish fit nicely with the fact that he harbored a trio of consecutive regrets that he felt had set the course of his life.

The first was a fact of nature and therefore was beyond the old man's control. Typically, it regarded the size of his penis. It was of average length and girth for his stature, which was slightly under average; the organ itself therefore was slightly smaller than average. In his youth he had sought out petite women specifically to match his condition. The old man had absorbed all the science and all the popular literature on the subject. No woman had ever come right out and complained, though three women, one in high school and two in the man's twenties, had brought up the subject of their own accord (based partly on misinformation). Nothing that any lover, physician, psychiatrist, or self-help author had ever said could deprive the old man of this crushing regret. Decades of great sex with beautiful, intelligent women had failed to erase the old man's conviction that every one of his lovers would have preferred a tall man with a huge cock and a prodigious ejaculation to go along with it. The confidence well-endowed men enjoyed affected every aspect of their lives, from the bedroom to the boardroom. That many such men were complete assholes was beside the point.

The old man's second regret was tied to his first, but only coincidentally. Of the hundreds of friends, colleagues, and acquaintances who had populated the old man's life, there was only one person he truly wished he had never met. In 1963, his senior year of college, after which he expected to marry his high-school sweetheart, he fell head over heels in love with another classmate. That he was still susceptible to this emotional upheaval told the man that he had no business marrying anyone just yet, and he broke off his engagement. In later years the man acknowledged that his marriage would have been a disaster anyway, for reasons that had nothing to do with the other woman. But the interloper's appearance in his life so overwhelmed him that he put his career on hold for a year. Eventually the man wasted a quarter of a century carrying the torch for this unfaithful siren, who in their earliest days together had tried to tell him that she was no good and that he should run in the opposite direction—if not necessarily back to his teenager and the dubious institution of marriage, at least into the light of sanity. The physically gorgeous creature was greedy, selfish, materialistic, shallow, mean, petty, vindictive, hypocritical, racist, xenophobic, and, as would follow from the foregoing, semiliterate and deeply religious. Indeed she had inspired the man's brief exploration of Catholicism. She was the second of the three women who had drawn attention to the man's undersized penis; she even had compared it derisively to her previous lover's. This devastating cruelty was insufficient to kill the man's crusading love.

At the height of their long affair, the couple spent four days at a mountain resort where they indulged in nonstop sex, dining, massage therapy, lounging in a hot tub, and other sensual delights. The man commemorated this tryst in the form of *Eight Autumn Poems,* the three of which that were not pornographic appear below:

October Mountain

You are to me as a great and lonely mountain.
Outside my window you are near and full of comfort;
As I walk this valley I embrace you.
But the journey to your summit is
Long and pricked with chance.
And whereas I have traversed these green fields and
Climbed tripping over your mossy rocks and
Drunk your ancient smells and reverberations
Thousands of times,
Still I little know you.

Each year I move my house closer to you,
That I may feel your low shudders in my bed,
That in my walks I may step surely
Amid your threatening vibrations,
That one day I may live in the center of your crown
And bathe in the everlasting glory
Of your liquid fire.

Your Eyes

When you seize me with your eyes,
When you envelop me in their
Transparent blue infinity,
I am as a man facing the hour of extinction,
As if time has been ordered still
And the planets' rotations halted
And the seasons' withering progress voided;
And when I no longer can endure your power
And I wrench away my gaze,
I am as a bee who in defending his queen
Rips out his strength and stumbles away
In stupid perfect fulfillment.

Your Kiss

Your kiss is my dearest surprise of late.
For so long it had been unformed and
Complacent and sadly forgetful.
But when we went away

From city, from work, from friends,
And from him,
Your kiss renewed itself and us;
And even in the cool darkness of autumn
Your kiss reminded of spring,
Of an April afternoon so long ago
When we were young
And he was someone else
And our future held such promise.

The old man's third and most irksome regret regarded the stunted career he ascribed to exhibit B. The romantic events of 1963 had prevented the man's relocating to New York, where as a playwright he would have stood a far better chance of success than he stood by remaining in a small suburban town.

Forty years later, in 2003, the old man attended a bucolic writers' conference where he met an agent who claimed to be friends with film director Martin Scorsese's housekeeper. The old man gave the agent a copy of his latest play, one of several works of his that the old man considered worthy of the big screen. None of the normal channels had ever opened any doors for him, and the supposed acquaintance of a famous person's domestic staff could not serve him any worse than he had served himself. As expected, he heard nothing more from the agent or her dubious connection.

One afternoon in the year 2014, the old man, aged seventy-two, stood naked before his bedroom mirror, envisioning his list of failures and disappointments as a long scroll of toilet tissue winding throughout the rooms of his apartment. This of course recalled the manuscript of Jack Kerouac's *On the Road* and the days when such an eccentric could still get an appointment with someone worth knowing in the publishing business. The old man stared at a reflection that looked at least fifteen years younger than it was, thanks to good genes and a lifetime of rigorous exercise. He estimated that he could look forward to ten, maybe even twenty more years of missed opportunities, broken promises, and unpublished plays.

The old man turned away from the mirror, sat down at his computer, went online, and ordered two matching handguns and a box of ammunition. Weeks later a well-read police detective would speculate that the paired firepower honored the self-inflicted punishment of Oedipus, the old man's favorite tragic character.

When the package arrived, the old man, having never even held a gun, much less fired one, read the owner's manual carefully. He loaded both pistols and placed them on his desk. He gathered up all his dormant manuscripts and threw them into his bathtub. He pocketed his wallet and car keys, wrapped the two guns inside a paper grocery sack, and doused the manuscripts with lighter fluid. He took a last look around the apartment, struck a match, and dropped it into the tub. He watched the flames for a while until he was certain they would not spread throughout his or anyone else's home. Then he walked out the front door, leaving it unlocked.

The old man drove an hour into the country, to a small state park that was never crowded even during the height of tourist season. He left his car in the parking lot and walked about a mile into the woods. He sat at the base of an old oak tree, cocked the pistols, and aimed. A grinning moment of gallows humor came over him as he stared into the twin barrels: *Well, now, here's something you don't see every day.*

A park ranger located the old man's body nine days later after noticing an abandoned car in the empty lot. The back of his skull and much of its rotting contents were fused to the bark of the tree.

Police found nothing of importance in the old man's apartment except the charred remains of his life's work in the bathtub. The only interesting item discovered on the cell phone he had left behind was a week-old text message from Martin Scorsese.

WATCHING HIS LANGUAGE

*S*eymour Putz Jr. was an analyst at the Central Intelligence Agency's headquarters in Langley, Virginia. Seymour served under presidents Truman, Eisenhower, Kennedy, Johnson, Nixon, and Ford and therefore experienced the "glory days" of the Cold War. Seymour's respectable and thoroughly uncontroversial career was a tribute to his father, Seymour Sr., who had risen from poverty in the mountains near Wheeling, West Virginia, to become a successful butcher in what then was rural Tysons Corner, Virginia. Seymour Jr. stayed close to his parents but rarely subjected his friends to their embarrassing backwoods ways.

To escape his pedigree and as an antidote to his tedious job, Seymour Jr. took up classical music as his personal medicine. His enviable LP collection, alphabetized by composer, eventually occupied two entire walls of his den and embraced every period from the Middle Ages to the early twentieth century. Seymour had no use for serialism, chance music, or other "arbitrary" styles of composition, but otherwise his taste was eclectic. To ensure variety, Seymour listened to his LPs in alphabetical order. (He kept this arbitrary inconsistency to himself.) He would come home from work, kiss the wife, lower the stylus on that evening's supper music, pour a respectable and uncontroversial glass of Scotch, and ease into his listening chair for the precisely thirty minutes that would elapse before Palestrina, Beethoven, or Stravinsky would be interrupted by the tinkling of a little bronze bell from the dining room. Often Seymour spent the rest of the night back in his den, cruising the collection until bedtime. He had read Donald Jay Grout's *History of Western Music* cover to cover twice and routinely bought the newest edition of the *Stereo Record Guide*. After retirement, Seymour took a music-appreciation course at new Northern Virginia Community College, only to discover that he knew the repertoire better than his young teacher did.

Seymour had met his wife, Carissimi Benedetto, as a lad vacationing in Venice. He had gone there to attend an early-music festival at San Marco; Carissimi was a clerk in a nearby record shop. The pretty brunette was studying English and welcomed Seymour's systematic tutoring. Their whirlwind romance provided decades of nostalgic family conversation. Whereas Seymour resented the years of cruel jokes his unfortunate name had inspired, Carissimi learned to deflect lewd references to her married version. Her own medicine was gardening, and she turned their modest home in McLean into a neighborhood showpiece. The couple raised an adorable daughter, Piccola.

One ancestral trait Seymour Jr. had failed to outrun was the salty vocabulary he had inherited from his dad. Although he was not a physically violent man, Seymour had a quick temper and at the slightest provocation could uncork a streak of working-class profanity that would shock family, friends, and colleagues. Whether it was a paper cut or the latest ridiculous bureaucratic policy, Seymour's tongue embarrassed everyone within earshot. Carissimi had tried without success to wean her husband of this ugly habit, and more than one co-worker had warned Seymour to watch his language.

Finally one afternoon Seymour's supervisor called him on the carpet and explained that his swearing in the workplace must cease. Seeking a peaceful solution, department head Robert Seidenberg asked Seymour to name his favorite pastime.

"Classical music, sir," Seymour answered proudly. "I listen every day, and my wife and I attend concerts whenever we can."

"Good, excellent," Seidenberg said. He sat back and looked out the window at the rolling Virginia countryside. "Here's an idea, Seymour," he continued. "From now on, whenever you find yourself about to use an obscene word, substitute the name of a famous composer."

Seymour stared at his boss for a moment as if the latter were engulfed in flames. "Uh, sure. Yes, sir." Then Seymour warmed to the idea; he had a penchant for puns anyway. "I'm *Abel* to *Handel* that," he offered experimentally, to Seidenberg's vague grin. "It won't happen again, sir."

And it did not. Seymour took Seidenberg's advice to heart and cleaned up his lexicon overnight. He made a project out of it, allowing revered musical names to pinch-hit for oaths, epithets, and even inoffensive words.

The next morning at work, Seymour lifted his coffee mug from a stack of papers to discover that the mug had left a stain on the top sheet. "Buxtehude!" he exclaimed.

"*Gesundheit!*" replied the analyst at the next desk.

Listening to the radio in the background, Seymour echoed President Eisenhower's objection to the growing influence of the military-industrial complex. *A really bad Delius,* Seymour thought.

Standing around a small television screen a few years thereafter with a group of colleagues watching Nikita Khrushchev lecture a smiling President Kennedy, Seymour mumbled, "That dirty son of a Binchois. *We will Berio,* indeed."

"Karl Ditters von Dittersdorf!" Seymour shouted the next morning in his living room after stepping barefoot on one of Piccola's Barbie dolls. No one else was home at the time, but Seymour had told Carissimi about his courteous new protocol. She would have giggled and made up a story to mollify Piccola when the child discovered the catastrophe. Seymour simply tossed the broken toy into the trash.

When his wife asked him later that day what they should serve their guests at an upcoming obligatory dinner, Seymour answered, "I don't give a flying Forqueray!"

Deciding to join in the fun, Carissimi suggested they take in a movie that evening, "just for the Halévy."

Seymour later declared *The Sound of Music* to be a piece of pure Korngold.

That weekend, Seymour hit his thumbnail with a hammer while repairing a window screen and screamed, "Godowsky to Hellmesberger!"

Back at work, having learned that President Johnson's

civil-rights bill would pass, Seymour mused, "It would Dufay all the odds if that made everyone Glazunov." Later, when a colleague told him about a new feature of their federal health insurance, Seymour agreed, "That's Gounod." After another staffer announced his plan to run for municipal office, Seymour congratulated him on his Fauré into politics. He agreed to ride in the candidate's convertible during a holiday parade. When the car developed engine trouble in the middle of the street, Seymour conjectured it was a bad Piston. The colleague later asked Seymour to proofread one of his campaign speeches, but the analyst complained that he could not read his pal's infernal Scriabin.

One Friday, Carissimi hired a sitter, called the office, and invited her husband to meet her after work for a drink. Two rounds later, Seymour reported that he felt a bit Galuppi. Listening to the bar's background music, Carissimi asked Seymour what he thought of this new pop group the Beatles—she herself considered the band positively Weill. Seymour replied that he did not mind their records but that he would never waste four dollars on one of their concerts, since no one could hear them over the Rore of the crowd. He pointed out that, given the Fab Four's influence on fashion, it was getting hard to Telemann from a woman. The nosy bartender turned the conversation to college football, and Seymour voiced his opinion of a promising new quarterback. Seymour considered the player overrated and thought his school might have to Swieten the deal. The bartender declined to weigh in on the matter. "Come on," Seymour persisted, "you can Tallis." The analyst decided that their barman was a crashing Borodin. Left alone finally, the couple commiserated on the ins and outs of family life. Seymour concluded that he was happy with their only daughter, despite Carissimi's tipsy suggestion that they Addison.

Staggering home afterward, Seymour and Carissimi were accosted by a smelly old beggar. "Schumann," Seymour said as they stepped around him.

Sniffling at his desk on Monday morning, Seymour feared he had picked up a cold; or perhaps he was allergic to some airborne Spohr. He also was bothered by a Krenek in his neck. "Shostakovich!" he exclaimed.

"*Gesundheit!*" replied the analyst at the next desk.

Seymour's department hosted a series of seminars for visiting foreign intelligence officers, three of which meetings were recorded by a technician named Larry and the other three by Larry's partner, Roger. Asked which set of tapes sounded better, Seymour reported that he preferred the Roger Sessions.

That Saturday morning, while Piccola was watching a cartoon cowboy perform rope tricks, Seymour wondered aloud whether the little guy knew the Orlando di Lasso. When later his daughter asked for a candy bar within an hour of lunch, Seymour said that would be a Nono. The devoted dad ordered Piccola to stop picking at the tiny scab on her leg and assured her that it would not leave a Scarlatti.

When President Johnson caved to his generals' pleas to step up the war in Vietnam, Seymour exclaimed, "Kreisler on a crutch! I swear to Gottschalk, that Texan is one D'Oyly Sammartini."

In 1972, President Nixon shook Mao Tse-tung's hand

on a slightly larger TV screen as Seymour said under his breath, "What a Chaminade. Yeah, you smile *now,* you miserable piece of Scheidt."

When the Watergate burglary came to light, Seymour let out a Graun, called the participants a bunch of amateurish Muffats, and hoped the cops would at least Khachaturian.

Seymour nearly slipped up at work one day a few years later when he told a colleague that nonstop media coverage of Nixon's resignation was really pissing him Offenbach. Now, having seen the president's dark side in the harsh Glière of news cameras, the rest of the country would have to clean up his Messiaen.

Quaker had just introduced its new "all-natural" cereal when Seymour observed a young intern in the staff lounge finishing a bowl of Granados. As she stood, Seymour noted to himself that she had a nice Heine.

When President Ford pardoned his predecessor, Seymour called the new commander in chief a Babbitting fool and announced his own retirement. He marched into Robert Seidenberg's office, took up a place on the Satie, and said he had had enough of this Bullock. "Sir Ernest," he clarified, responding to Seidenberg's look of annoyance. "English organist, not much of a composer, really."

"Right," replied Seidenberg. He looked over his employee's resignation letter and handed it back to him. "Now get the Fux out of here!"

At his desk, as he prepared to sign the Photostat, Seymour pricked his finger on a staple. "Tchaikovsky!" he exclaimed.

"*Gesundheit!*" replied the analyst at the next desk.

WOMEN

From a diary found at the top of the Key West Lighthouse

First look, 1957

G., the girl across the street, my age, six. Blonde, blue eyes, cute. My best friend by default: she was the only other young kid in our sparsely populated neighborhood. We developed an intense curiosity about each other's person, which we indulged in a secret meeting behind the toolshed in her backyard. Fascinated by our different equipment, standing six feet apart. This single viewing led to innocent doctor exams and mock spankings, nothing vaguely sexual since we knew nothing of sex. G.'s mom was mean to her, which may have explained the hiding place and the fact that G. would have to repeat the first grade. Never saw the dad, if he was around. I was proud of myself for not judging or rejecting G. But when surprisingly she telephoned me six years later, during the seventh grade, I was too embarrassed to return her call. Pubescent stupidity. I'm sorry, G.

First kiss, 1962

J. lived down the street; we played sports and sledded together with other boys and girls. Again, same grade, blonde, blue eyes, cute, but sort of a tomboy, and an inch or so taller than I. No hint of attraction until one summer evening when I walked her home and we stood on her porch in a sudden awkward silence. She smiled at me under the moth-buzzing lamp and seemed in no hurry to go inside. Confused but convinced that J. was expecting me to do something, I reached up on tiptoe and kissed her lightly on the cheek. A fantastic spark of newness, a creature from another land, a rush of sweet-smelling hair, soft skin, a barely audible sigh. J. blushed, smiled, and went in. We never spoke of it or touched each other again, though we remained friends. We must have known we were physically mismatched. But what a moment.

First kiss on the lips, 1962

C. lived directly across the street. Looked a bit like Shirley Temple, with the same tight sunny ringlets. A year or two younger than I, my best friend's sister's best friend, and I'd always regarded C. as a little kid. That is, until the morning when she showed up in her pajamas outside my bedroom window and called me out to play. We liked to frolic in and under the apple tree in her backyard and sample the fruit. Today that screams out as a biblical cliché, but of course we had no such thoughts. The summer morning when C. was skipping about under the tree in her PJs, raising an intriguing line of dewdrops above her upper lip, I noticed a slightly provocative change in her demeanor; suddenly she seemed more my age. We confessed our curiosity about grown-up kissing and arranged to discover it for ourselves. Her next-door neighbors, our best friends, had an industrious father who had built them a big wooden backyard playhouse shaped and painted like Kennedy's PT boat; this had become the neighborhood meeting place. C. and I gathered there in the twilight, knelt across from each other on the hard, sweet-smelling pine boards, and awaited the courage to move closer. I was masking my own fear when I asked her what she was afraid of, to which she answered, "Nothing." Thus cornered, I leaned in, took her little fairy's face in my hands, and kissed her lightly but lingeringly on the lips. We didn't think to open our mouths, embrace, or otherwise pursue each other. We merely knelt there afterward smiling, having moved into a new dimension.

First French kiss, 1963

C., not the same girl as C. above, also lived down the street; J. above lived next door. C. was what you'd call my first long-term girlfriend, though our term consisted mainly of one summer. Like the other C., this C. was adventurous; one afternoon after school she challenged me to show-and-tell. A creek ran through our neighborhood, into which a series of huge concrete pipes emptied rainwater. You could bend over and walk for miles in those pipes; you'd stop to tell stories or misbehave under the occasional manhole cover, where the pipe was wide enough for you to stand upright in and where the light was better. Except after a rainstorm there was only a trickle of water at the bottom of the pipes at any given time. C. and I went in that afternoon and walked until we were sure we couldn't be seen from either direction. We sat next to each other in the chilly dampness and giggled at our, rather, her mission. C. was dying for me to see her down there, and to see me. I was equally curious about her but terrified at the prospect of presenting myself. We had not kissed or touched, and I was completely soft. But I loved C. and would have done anything she asked. So she pulled out her waistband and showed me her little wisp of light-brown fur, the important bits beneath which I could not see well in the half-light, and I showed her my all-too-obvious bits, displayed in their least important condition. Thus satisfied, C. smiled. Then she shivered slightly, which gave me the opportunity to suggest we reemerge into the warm sunlight. There we indulged in a long, stimulating embrace, silently acknowledging that we couldn't wait to get our hands on each other. Which we did, many times, always while fully dressed, hiding in her rec room or mine or in a movie theater. I had admitted to C. that I had begun masturbating; she either hadn't or wasn't ready to own up to it. We never tried to make each other come; that would have been messy and *too* grown-up. But one evening on her back porch, C.'s best friend, M., challenged us to a similarly forbidden act called the French kiss. M.'s description sounded slightly gross, but we were glad to be her guinea pigs. M. as an audience was not uninteresting. The kiss was sweet and delightful and a little scary, an opening to other unthinkable crimes. But C. and I never went further than that. We kissed endlessly and touched endlessly and drove each other to distraction all summer long. One night I was privileged to thank our M. for her inspiration during a session of spin the bottle.

First oral sex, 1967

I fell madly in love with K. at the community pool. Smashing: a miniature Sophia Loren. We progressed quickly to giddy viewings of each other and more serious petting. Still pre-orgasmic: she too knew I masturbated but had not admitted to it herself. She tried a few times to jack me off, without success, this failure more the result of our typically rushed, guilty rendezvous than of K.'s inexperience. But the day she finally took me in her mouth was a burst of wild pleasure as unforgettable as it was brief. I went down on her with equal fascination; K.'s self-consciousness melted away as I addressed her womanhood with the ignorance of my fifteen years. K. and I were forcibly separated at summer's end when my family moved away: the most agonizing event of my youth. We remained close, eventually met other people, drifted apart, and reunited many years later, completing our unfinished business in spectacular fashion. We're friends today, though we are political opposites and possibly would strangle each other if given the chance.

First hand job, 1968

I dislike the term *hand job,* as I do *blow job* and *pussy* and other crude sexual terms—though *pussy* and *fuck* can sound nice in a breathless woman's voice. I had heard *blow job* many times before I ever heard its manual equivalent. Pubescent guys had called it *jacking off;* whatever girls called their own masturbation was another of life's crystalline mysteries. (The overheard term *flicking her clit* meant nothing to me at the time because of my inadequate sexual training.) I didn't hear the boorish *jerking off* until a European friend used it years later in his worldly hometown. The next year, my expatriate American friends were calling it *beating off:* uglier still, but that was the term of use. So it was that one afternoon in a forest the fabulous love of my life, L., with whom I had practiced all the skills learned to date, lowered my pants as we lay passionately kissing and asked in her sweet freshman voice, "Would you like me to beat you off?" We laughed simultaneously, both at the repulsive term and at the life-altering door she had opened. I don't remember exactly how I replied—she probably does—but it was something to the effect of, "Sure!" What next took place was an act so tender, intuitive, and full of invincible young love that it will live forever in our hearts. L. had never even seen a penis before our meeting, but somehow she treated mine like her favorite teddy bear. When after several minutes I realized I was going to come, it felt like first communion. Doing that alone was miraculous enough; doing it in a girl's presence, as a result of her dedication, was like diving off a cliff. L. knew nothing of the stages of arousal, and I felt it was simple courtesy to warn her of the impending explosion. L. removed her left hand from its feathery assistance and cupped it in front of me. Astonished at our intimacy, I lay back and gave myself over to her. L.'s cries of surprise and excitement echo in my ears as I type this. No rough footballer had told L. how to react; she simply finished me off better than I ever had done myself. Afterward she smiled up at me and spent a long time examining the eagerly anticipated product of our hunger. Eventually she poured it onto a nearby fallen leaf and continued staring at it in amazement. That handful would be the first of many L. would draw from me at least once a day for semesters to come.

First blow job, 1969

As a term, *fellatio* isn't much of an improvement, so I'll stick with the vernacular. I should call this the first *complete* blow job, since at least two other girls had taken me in their mouths inconclusively—just as I had yet to learn how to make a girl come that way. J., not the same as J. above, had taught herself to jack me off nearly as well as L. and likewise had learned to play catch. This had as much to do with those mostly dressed meetings in secret places as with J.'s sense of decorum. Finally one day she decided instead to catch me in her mouth. She did the main work with her hands, but adding her pouting lips was an act of generosity too good to refuse. Afterward she showed it to me and teased it around with her tongue before releasing it into a sink conveniently installed in her bedroom closet. One day several untidy mouthfuls later, J., tired of breaking the mood, made a great show of swallowing me. Finally I understood what Mark Twain meant by eyes that snapped.

First intercourse, 1969

Another J., but neither of the above; I'm committed to authenticity, however thinly disguised. This J. and I were just friends, not lovers. We were high-school seniors living temporarily in Europe. She had a boyfriend in the country next door, and my girlfriend had returned to America. J. was a petite, well-endowed blonde who actually didn't attract me until the day we found ourselves alone in the senior lounge talking about sex. Neither of us had progressed beyond mutual masturbation, and we sensed that most of our friends had moved on to intercourse; we were mistaken. But our stimulating afternoon talks became a ritual, and eventually one day we decided to find out what all the fuss was about. A male friend had told me that the cleaning staff never checked behind the curtains in the ground-floor senior lounge and that you could unlatch a window late in the day and sneak back in after dark with a girl. If the sofas in that room could talk! J. and I rode the public bus from her stop back to school; as promised, the window yielded to my gentle push. J. and I climbed in, took a deep breath, and wondered how to proceed. We decided to undress each other. We hadn't even kissed, but it was a good decision. Each of us would be the first person of the opposite sex the other had seen completely naked. She looked lovely in the streetlight that filtered through the curtains, and I was already rock-hard when J. undid my jeans. We embraced, my erection pulsating hotly between us. Finally we made out for a while until we had the vague sense that we were ready for the main event. I had bought a small packet of condoms—I recounted to J. the humiliating pharmacy interview required in those days—and presented it to her mutual fascination. We decided it would be more meaningful for her to roll it on, which she did with a smile; that part, at least, felt pretty good. Then she lay back on the sofa and opened her beautiful legs. I lay over her, she took me in her hand, and I slipped right into her. She moaned convincingly, but all I felt of J. was diffused warmth. Instinctively we began moving, and her enjoyment seemed genuine; it was all I could do to hide my disappointment. After many minutes, J.'s breathing suddenly sped up and she pushed against me with all her might. Still clueless regarding a woman's anatomy, I could only hope that she had come. I certainly was nowhere near that stage myself, and, after J. had settled back down somewhat, we took the opportunity to explore the other positions we had heard about. We enjoyed all of them, especially the one where she rode me as I sat up; facing me was better than the other direction, though each had its charms. Finally J. confessed to fatigue, and both of us accepted the fact that the condom was a drag. I knelt before her and watched her free my yearning cock. Without a word she directed me down on my back and lay beside and across me on the narrow cushions. J. used only one hand because her other was trapped beneath us, but our long intercourse had served as dynamic foreplay. In a few minutes I showered us both; kissing her forehead as she lavished herself on me I felt it land in our hair. Later that term we enjoyed a few manual get-togethers but didn't revisit our new adventure; privately each of us must have known it would improve with a romantic partner. We did have intercourse again, about ten times during a single weekend, the following year when it turned out that our stateside colleges were reasonably near to each other. But I was young and selfish and did not part with J. on respectable terms. I will carry that shame to my grave.

Second intercourse, 1971

As expected, making love with a girlfriend rather than a mere fellow researcher was another thing altogether. My first time with L., the love of my life, was her first time and was precisely as wonderful as everyone had said it was supposed to be. We had explored each other as fully as we knew how, and by her eighteenth birthday L. was as hungry for intercourse as I. She had learned to masturbate using a pillow on a chair and wasted no time describing it to me. She even had made herself come riding my butt bone one day on the floor of my Volkswagen Bus, sweetly sharing her trust and dissolving inhibition. She felt her initiative was embarrassing and slightly weird, but I would gladly have offered her the gearshift for the same purpose. One day not long thereafter, sitting on the backseat of the Bus with my head in her lap, L. announced that she was ready to take me inside her. "Oh, yes," she smiled, flexing her gorgeous ass, "I want to *do* it!" We drove to our favorite cornfield and let nature take its course. We were so deeply in love and so ravenous that we rejected out of hand the idea of using a condom. This was long before AIDS, but we had not yet learned that I didn't necessarily need to ejaculate inside her to start a family. We were lucky—for years, as it would happen. She loved it from the first moment, and I was amazed at how she, my girl, felt with nothing between us. She didn't come that day, though she would learn how, usually on top. That time and many times thereafter I withdrew at the last moment and she gave me her knowing hand, each of us luxuriating in the long streams that adorned her beautiful young body. Eventually L. went on the pill and we learned the next level of ecstasy. In a few years I had come in and on nearly every part of her, but that intense oneness of filling L. as she sighed and moaned with joy was like nothing else.

First hands-free blow job, 1973

By now several girls had made me come in their mouths using mostly their hands. But T., a diva in every sense of the word, was especially proud of her oral powers. She disliked swallowing, but she was always ready to take me to heaven with her coloratura while freeing her hands for other purposes. I mention this mainly because to this point I had regarded the blow job as highly overrated and doubted that any woman would ever make me come that way without basically jacking me off into her mouth. In this as in many other matters of the flesh, I would be happily corrected. I am sorry to admit further that it was T., following several years of uneducated bliss with more deserving girls, who instructed me on the ways of the clitoris. She was the first woman I was able to make come orally and by every other means, and her orgasm was as operatic as everything else she did. Unfortunately, what I took from her lessons was the wish that I could turn back the clock and share my diploma with all those other girls.

These male-oriented milestones have little to do with love or with the complex emotions that women bring to the bedroom. The diarist appears to have been a good listener and, usually, a gentleman who brought many women happiness and who managed to distribute his DNA around the globe without increasing its overpopulation. Marginal notes confirm that the diarist regarded women as nature's finest creation. His opinion was that there would be a great deal less war, corruption, illiteracy, hunger, disease, and general stupidity in the world if more women were allowed to climb on top. It is inevitable that they will, but it may be too late for this particular planet. In the meantime, let the diarist's phallic riffing serve as a salute, a small expression of hope.

Thank you for reading.
Please review this book. Reviews help others find
Absolutely Amazing eBooks and inspire us to keep
providing these marvelous tales.

If you would like to be put on our email list to receive
updates on new releases, contests, and promotions, please
go to AbsolutelyAmazingEbooks.com and sign up.

ACKNOWLEDGMENTS

I thank the Anne McKee Artists Fund of the Florida Keys, Inc., for its support; I thank Key West High School teacher Valerie Mathijsen-Palay for polishing my rusty French; I thank my sister, Carol Pittard, for remembering Effie's name; and I thank those members of the Florida Keys arts community who strive to maintain the high standards of "the real world."

ABOUT THE AUTHOR

Hal Howland is the author of *After Jerusalem: A Story and Two Novellas, The Human Drummer: Thoughts on the Life Percussive, The Jazz Buyer: Short Fiction,* and *Landini Cadence and Other Stories,* a finalist in the 2011 Next Generation Indie Book Awards and a recipient of the 2012 Eric Hoffer Award for excellence in independent publishing. Howland's work has been nominated for the Lorian Hemingway Short Story Competition, *Short Story America,* the *Writer's Digest* Popular Fiction Awards, and other honors. Howland has released three award-winning, critically acclaimed jazz recordings, *The Howland Ensemble, Reiko,* and *10 Years in 5 Days,* and has received a jazz fellowship from the National Endowment for the Arts. Born in Washington, D.C., and raised in Virginia, Europe, and the Middle East, Howland lives in Key West, Florida. His Web site address is www.halhowland.com.

PRAISE FOR *AFTER JERUSALEM*

"'Murder in the Percussion Section' [is] a gourmet trip through the percussion kitchen—accessories and all!" **Fred Begun**, principal timpanist emeritus, National Symphony Orchestra

"Hal Howland is a great observer of human nature. He has an uncanny ability to get right to the heart of matters with a dry and subtle wit." **Andrea Comstock**, executive director, Key West Art Center

"Entertaining!" **Peter Erskine**, jazz drummer

"One hell of a read! A real page-turner, enriched by Howland's wry sense of humor and twisted imagination. Characters [are] vividly drawn, [with] possibly the most considerate episodes of sexual congress ever recorded: warm and real and attractive. Hard-hitting action, suspense, and sweeping local color aplenty. Howland's voice is strong, gripping, and laugh-out-loud funny. After Jerusalem is a trip: pick it up and buckle your seat belt." **Constance Gilbert**, *Solares Hill*

"Hal Howland weaves a tale that is reminiscent of when short stories flourished in magazines and publishers fought each other for writers' stories. Howland brings the Key West I know so well to life and captures the essence of the characters that call the end of the road home. Howland's weaving of his knowledge of music through the stories is masterful. I not only enjoyed the stories, but

closed the book having learned something too." **Michael Haskins**, author of *Chasin' the Wind*

"*Hal Howland mixes musical mystery, sexual mayhem, and foreign intrigue into a literary treat of symphonic proportions. Bravo!*" **Michael Suib**, author and former *Miami Herald* columnist

Praise for *The Human Drummer*

"*Bravissimo! What a wonderful achievement. This is a great contribution to what we are all about.*" **Fred Begun**, principal timpanist emeritus, National Symphony Orchestra

"*Really enjoyed it very much! Hal has obviously done his homework. Great reading, understandable, and should be in every musician's library.*" **Hal Blaine**, studio drummer

"*Hal must be congratulated! He offers much wisdom into the performer's life and the realities of the business. Young drummers would find it inspiring.*" **Tony Cirone**, principal percussionist, San Francisco Symphony Orchestra

"*Opens the drummer's world to everyone!*" **Britt Conley**, Washington drummer-photographer

"*With a distinctive, personal writing voice, classical and jazz percussionist Hal Howland presents the ABCs of* making a life in music and, by extension, in any of the arts. Professional musicians as well as music students and their parents will find solid advice about day jobs, fitness, and equipment care, among many other things, as well as Howland's extensive research on timpani. General-interest readers can enjoy Howland's musical memories and informed opinions as well as his interviews with drummers John Densmore of the Doors and Graeme Edge of the Moody Blues. Reference sections include a professional directory and an irreverent but useful glossary." CUA Magazine

"Very interesting! Glad to know that my name is mentioned among such notables." **Andrew Cyrille**, avant-garde jazz drummer

"Fills a niche! Says many things of interest to both drummers and laypersons, entertaining, explains the everyday world of the working musician, substantial—there is an interested readership out there for this book." **Peter Erskine**, drummer and leader

"Compelling, humorous—I can offer only words of praise!" **Chet Falzerano**, drum historian

"Wow! Talk about comprehensive. I also like his very 'human' approach to all his subjects." **Vic Firth**, former solo timpanist, Boston Symphony Orchestra

"Informative, witty, entertaining, reflective, and realistic!" **Jim Lambert**, Percussive Notes

"Truly a masterpiece, and every drummer should read it! Nothing like it has ever been written. It is a wonderful piece of literature: his command of the language is magnificent and the ideas expressed in such flowing narrative as to retain the reader's interest throughout. A work for the ages." **William F. Ludwig Jr.**, drum manufacturer

"Very enjoyable, very well written!" **Chet McCracken**, drummer, the Doobie Brothers

"Progressive thinkers like Hal are exactly what we need!" **Alfonso Pollard**, Washington freelancer and union activist

"Intelligent and to the point! There's a lot to learn from this book." **Harry Schroeder**, *Solares Hill*

"Eminently readable!" **Rick Van Horn**, former senior editor, *Modern Drummer* magazine

"I couldn't put it down! It just blows me away." **Roger "Hurricane" Wilson**, blues guitarist

"A masterpiece! I love it. As a teacher, I need to know this." **Ginger Zyskowski**, owner, Professional Drum School, Hutchinson, Kansas

Praise for *The Jazz Buyer*

"The book contains a diverse body of fiction with some wildly imaginative plot lines, many of them dusted with the dark glitter of Howland's unique narrative voice as a sexy, deliciously twisted, but unfailingly polite bad boy. Howland takes the old 'sex and drugs and rock and roll' to a new and sophisticated height. A personal favorite remains the new edition of the lauded Israeli-Palestinian spy novella 'After Jerusalem,' which concludes this latest work. The Jazz Buyer *is a clever, erotic winner!"* **Connie Gilbert**, *Solares Hill*

Praise for *Landini Cadence*

"It's great! It kept me guessing till the end." **Larry Erskine**, Key West city attorney

"Just started reading Hal Howland's Landini Cadence, *and it is easy to see this is another runaway Key West hit for him! His Rich Castillo, the homicide detective who moonlights as a drummer, is a winner. Loved his conversation with the racist, holier-than-thou Pastor Pilcher after the murder of his two church members. Howland paints that area of the Lower Keys exactly as it is. Can't wait to read the rest of the book!"* **Peg Gregory**, author of *Starfish*

"What a fun book! A great example of the inspiration of love." **Michael Larson**, St. Peter Catholic Church choir director

"I love it! It grabs the reader from the first page and

doesn't let go. Read it twice!" **Howard Livingston**, singer-songwriter

"Howland's best piece of fiction yet! On its surface the novel is a well-structured work that fits cozily into the niche of crime fiction, a pitch-perfect poolside read that's amply disturbing and compelling. What sets it apart is its most unexpected gift: an unflinching look at the politics and customs at work in our sunny island chain." **Jennifer O'Lear**, author of *Pressure Drop*, in *Solares Hill*

"As a sex-crazed, gun-toting musician, I must say I found it enjoyable, all derogatory comments on the current state of conservatism aside!" **Tim Smyser**, bassist, Johnny & the Rebels

"Couldn't put the book down once I started it!" **Adrienne Zolondick**, singer-songwriter

The New
Atlantian Library

NewAtlantianLibrary.com
or AbsolutelyAmazingeBooks.com
or AA-eBooks.com

www.ingramcontent.com/pod-product-compliance
Lightning Source LLC
Chambersburg PA
CBHW070447030726
47503CB00004B/935